Consider the Evidence

'You knock a chip off that bloody car and stop worrying about what you can't do.' Miller cut the connection.

Craig left the telephone kiosk. The drizzle had increased in intensity and he raised the collar of his mackintosh. He cursed Miller....

It could so easily turn out that Haggard had not done the Frindhurst job. Then, an illegal trespass to his goods would be doubly wrong. The fact that Haggard had never himself operated within the law was, in this context irrelevant.

He hesitated. If he returned to Frindhurst and said he'd stuck by the letter of the law, Dusty would swear, pick up the telephone, and ask someone in Telton to belt the Buick a sharp blow and so secure a sample of the paintwork. There was bound to be more than one policeman in Telton who would think, with Miller, that there was nothing wrong in such action. His own refusal to do as he had been ordered would result in a short delay, nothing more. He smiled briefly. Since when had virtue ever stood a ghost of a chance against vice?

He returned to the Buick and used his penknife to force off a chip of paint, which he put in the envelope of the last letter Daphne had written him. When he pocketed the envelope and turned, he saw an old tramp, standing on the pavement, watching.

Craig walked out of the forecourt. The tramp stood still, but his head moved round as he watched and water dripped unheeded from his torn and dirty cap on to his stubbled cheek.

JEFFREY
ASHFORD
Consider
The
Evidence

WALKER AND COMPANY · NEW YORK

DEC 0 8 1985

Copyright © 1966 by Jeffrey Ashford

All rights reserved. No part of this book may be reproduced or
transmitted in any form or by any means, electric or mechanical,
including photocopying, recording, or by any information storage
and retrieval system, without permission in writing from the
Publisher.

All the characters and events portrayed in this story are
fictitious.

First published in the United States of America in 1966 by the
Walker Publishing Company, Inc.

This paperback edition first published in 1985.

ISBN: 0-8027-3114-7

Library of Congress Catalog Card Number: 66-23929

Printed in the United States of America

10 9 8 7 6 5 4 3 2 1

Consider The Evidence

Other titles in the Walker British Mystery Series

Peter Alding • BETRAYED BY DEATH
Peter Alding • A MAN CONDEMNED
Peter Alding • MURDER IS SUSPECTED
Peter Alding • RANSOM TOWN
Jeffrey Ashford • THE HANDS OF INNOCENCE
Jeffrey Ashford • A RECIPE FOR MURDER
Jeffrey Ashford • SLOW DOWN THE WORLD
Jeffrey Ashford • THREE LAYERS OF GUILT
Pierre Audemars • GONE TO HER DEATH
Pierre Audemars • NOW DEAD IS ANY MAN
Marian Babson • DANGEROUS TO KNOW
Marian Babson • THE LORD MAYOR OF DEATH
Brian Ball • DEATH OF A LOW-HANDICAP MAN
Brian Ball • MONTENEGRIN GOLD
Josephine Bell • A QUESTION OF INHERITANCE
Josephine Bell • STROKE OF DEATH
Josephine Bell • TREACHERY IN TYPE
Josephine Bell • THE TROUBLE IN HUNTER WARD
Josephine Bell • VICTIM
Josephine Bell • WOLF! WOLF!
W.J. Burley • DEATH IN A SALUBRIOUS PLACE
W.J. Burley • DEATH IN STANLEY STREET
W.J. Burley • DEATH IN WILLOW PATTERN
W.J. Burley • TO KILL A CAT
W.J. Burley • THE SCHOOLMASTER
W.J. Burley • WYCLIFFE AND THE SCHOOLGIRLS
Desmond Cory • DEADFALL
Desmond Cory • THE NIGHT HAWK
Desmond Cory • TIMELOCK
Desmond Cory • UNDERTOW
John Creasey • THE BARON IN FRANCE
John Creasey • THE BARON AND THE UNFINISHED PORTRAIT
John Creasey • HELP FROM THE BARON
John Creasey • LAST LAUGH FOR THE BARON

John Creasey • THE TOFF AND THE FALLEN ANGELS
John Creasey • TRAP THE BARON
June Drummond • FUNERAL URN
June Drummond • SLOWLY THE POISON
William Haggard • A COOL DAY FOR KILLING
William Haggard • THE KINSMEN
William Haggard • MISCHIEF MAKERS
William Haggard • THE NOTCH ON THE KNIFE
William Haggard • THE POISON PEOPLE
William Haggard • THE SCORPION'S TAIL
William Haggard • TOO MANY ENEMIES
William Haggard • VISA TO LIMBO
William Haggard • YESTERDAY'S ENEMY
Simon Harvester • ASSASSIN'S ROAD
Simon Harvester • MOSCOW ROAD
Simon Harvester • ZION ROAD
J.G. Jeffreys • A CONSPIRACY OF POISONS
J.G. Jeffreys • A WICKED WAY TO DIE
J.G. Jeffreys • SUICIDE MOST FOUL
J.G. Jeffreys • THE WILFUL LADY
Elizabeth Lemarchand • CHANGE FOR THE WORSE
Elizabeth Lemarchand • CYANIDE WITH COMPLIMENTS
Elizabeth Lemarchand • NO VACATION FROM MURDER
Elizabeth Lemarchand • STEP IN THE DARK
Elizabeth Lemarchand • SUDDENLY WHILE GARDENING
Elizabeth Lemarchand • UNHAPPY RETURNS
Hugh McLeave • NO FACE IN THE MIRROR
Laurie Mantell • MURDER AND CHIPS
Laurie Mantell • A MURDER OR THREE
Emma Page • ADD A PINCH OF CYANIDE
John Sladek • BLACK AURA
John Sladek • INVISIBLE GREEN
Estelle Thompson • FIND A CROOKED SIXPENCE
Estelle Thompson • HUNTER IN THE DARK

1

THE cream coloured Buick Riviera stopped and was then neatly backed into the parking bay. Haggard climbed out and put a shilling into the parking meter. He returned to his seat behind the wheel.

'Five past,' said Brown.

Haggard looked at his wrist watch. He took a packet of Camel cigarettes from his coat pocket.

They watched the people on the pavements. The Odeon cinema, to the right of where they were parked, was showing a horror film, and outside, by the doors, was a cut-out monster, looking ludicrous in the warm sunlight. A uniformed constable was stopped by a woman with a small, bawling child and he pointed down the main street to the traffic lights. Several people entered the supermarket, next to the Odeon, where tomato soup was being sold at threepence a tin off.

Haggard took off his dark glasses and rubbed his eyes. He replaced the glasses. He drew on the cigarette and savoured the smoke with the extra pleasure that came from being not long out of prison, where cigarettes were always rolled, as thin as the lead in a pencil and every match was split into four.

He thought about the job. The Lip had guaranteed it would be worth the right side of thirty grand. Something like two for expenses, the usual twenty per cent for The Lip, and that left twenty-four. Six each. It would be something to feel the money rustling again. Man needed money. He needed it to keep the birds singing and perhaps for bunging the cozzpots if anything went wrong. His last spell in nick had come about only because the splits were stupid enough to be honest. A smart split knew that if he wanted to die rich it wasn't any use relying on his wages.

'Ten past,' said Brown.

Haggard looked at the bank doors. They were strong and elegantly simple, respectable doors for the respectable people who put their money inside. They'd lifted the money, but legally. The world was a jungle, but if you were really smart you always ran with the hunters. Then, all the money you nicked was legal. Amass enough of it and they made you so respectable they anointed you Sir or Lord or Duke. Make a million out of the sweat of others and you became Lord Muck and people rushed to shake your hand. He was reminded of the psychiatrist who'd seen him last time in the nick. A tall, thin man with as much real sympathy and understanding inside him as an undertaker's slab of marble.

'Good morning, Haggard, sit down there. Smoke? I thought we'd have a little chat and get to know each other. This isn't the first time you've been in prison, is it?'

Could he get any stupider than that? The papers were all in front of the man. Nine convictions. Everything in the book from juvenile delinquency to armed robbery. 'No, it's not the first time.' Call him a stupid bastard and he'd scream for the screws. That would mean up before the governor and a four, four, four: four days bread and water, four days loss of remission, four days loss of privileges. When you were inside, you couldn't win.

'You're obviously an intelligent man, Haggard. Don't you think it's a pity to waste all that intelligence by spending all your life in prison?'

'I've spent more time outside than inside.'

'But this is your ninth conviction.'

'It's an occupational hazard. Drive a lorry long enough and you crash: it's an occupational hazard.'

'I'm sure you don't really see it like that.'

'Are you telling me, or asking me?'

'Is it worth spending your best years in prison for the sake of a few small robberies?'

'I've made more out of it than you ever have, or the governor of this stinking jail. The last job brought in four thousand and I spent it inside three months. I met a couple of birds who were sensational: they'd have hung an L plate on Fanny Hill.'

At this point, the psychiatrist had begun to look a little sour. All psychiatrists, all prison ones that was, started off with the assumption that in every crooked man there was an honest man trying to get out. That showed just how much they didn't know. Every man was a crook by nature and it was the cowards who went straight.

'Now look here, Haggard, what about the future?'

'What about it? Unless the supply of birds is suddenly cut off, I'll live.'

'You won't always be young, you know.'

This bloke was a genius. Men appeared in the history books for being as clever as this.

'What will happen when you're older and want to settle down in a house of your own?'

'I'll take a couple of aspirins and lie down until the feeling passes.'

This militantly friendly man refused to be put off. 'You'll want to be married to a good woman.'

'I knew a good woman once upon a time. She died early, from boredom.'

'Wouldn't you like a family?'

'I've probably got several. I've just never stayed around long enough to find out.'

The psychiatrist lit a second cigarette and again offered Haggard one. 'Violence is a truly dreadful thing. It's the denial of civilisation.'

'So what's the H-bomb? Civilisation's favourite piece of propaganda?'

'Think about the poor man you hit so savagely with a crowbar: think how his life has been blasted by unnecessary violence.'

'Whose fault was it he got belted? He wanted to play the hero and blow his whistle so I had to hit the silly little bastard.'

Haggard's mind was jerked back to the present when Brown spoke. 'Here's the van,' said Brown.

They watched the armoured van, painted blue and red, come to a halt in front of the 'No Parking' sign by the bank. The uniformed driver and his companion climbed out of the cab and went round to the back. The driver unlocked the doors, which were then unbolted from the inside. Three more uniformed guards jumped down to the ground. They brought with them three metal cases and an Alsatian, on a lead. The driver stayed by the van while the other four went into the bank.

Haggard looked at his watch. Eleven-eighteen. In four weeks the time of the armoured van's arrival had not varied by more than five minutes. The Lip had guaranteed it wouldn't: the bank had to pay out so much money on Thursdays and Fridays that there was a very strict time-table for large withdrawals.

Haggard studied the van. Based on the 2¾-ton Austin commercial, it had been converted by a Midlands firm who boasted that their products were thief proof. The doors were bolted from the inside, all locks were extremely complicated, and the sides, back, and top of the van were made of armoured plate which would defy any portable oxy-acetylene equipment for a long time. But one of the workers at the small factory where the vans were converted had spoken up. The bulkhead dividing the cab from the cargo space was not of armoured plate: something to do with economy, weight, and balance. On the roof of the cab was a grill which marked the alarm: the claim was that when it went off it could be heard in hell.

Haggard looked at his watch again. Four minutes since the guards went inside. Very soon, they would be coming out with thirty thousand pounds, plus, in their hands. Even today, with inflation everywhere, thirty thousand sounded quite nice.

The four guards came out of the bank. The Alsatian was off the lead and walking with short, mincing steps as if waiting for a fight. The three guards with the money—the metal cases were now chained to them—were in front and the other guard, hand on truncheon, and the Alsatian were just behind them. Their truncheons had a small reservoir of liquid which could be sprayed out: the liquid blinded a man for several minutes— quite long enough for the Law to catch up with events.

The three guards with the money climbed into the back of the van, the Alsatian jumped inside, and the doors were locked. The fourth guard joined the driver in the cab. The metal grills were in position on the side windows: the grill of the windscreen would drop down at the touch of a button.

Haggard started the engine of the Buick.

The armoured van drew out a few inches from the pavement, waited until a heavy lorry had gone by and then continued out into the stream of traffic. It went up the High Street to the traffic lights, set at red.

Haggard let two private cars pass before he came out into the road and joined the waiting traffic. He told Brown to light him another fag. Having been out of prison for only a short time, he kept on smoking to prove to himself that he was at liberty to do so: after a while, this compulsion would pass and he'd reduce his intake to something like forty a day.

The lights changed and the traffic moved. The van went up the High Street to the X-shaped cross roads, divided by 'Keep Left' islands, and turned left down Quarrington Street, right at the end into Station Road. It passed over the railway bridge and maintained a steady thirty along Brooklyn Road, past the rows of terraced houses, the small clusters of shops, and the three churches of various denominations.

Brooklyn Road was a mile and a half long. It started on the outskirts of the business area of Frindhurst, travelled through the depressing 1910 housing estate, along the side of the new housing estate built in ugly yellow bricks, and ended by the conglomeration of buildings that had once been an asylum and was now a secondary modern school. At the T-junction, the van turned right. In the following Buick, Haggard braked to turn left and he brought the car to a halt along the road. He looked at his watch. Eleven-thirty-eight. A quick mental calculation told him that over the four weeks the average time taken to this point was $16\frac{1}{2}$ minutes.

'Everything's smooth,' said Brown, speaking for the first time during the journey.

'Let's keep it that way.' Haggard, ignoring a small Mini coming up fast from behind, drew out from the pavement.

The large American car blocked the road for the Mini, which had to brake sharply. The driver hooted.

Haggard drove down the first turning to the right, a road which had high blackthorn hedges on either side. It curved round and on the right was a lane, at the head of which was the sign 'No through road.'

Haggard stopped the car and climbed out. The sunlight caught his face and showed the deeply etched lines on it, lines far more frequent than would have normally been found on a man of thirty-three. He had light brown wavy hair, very blue eyes, a squarish nose, and very regular white teeth. There was a scar on his cheek, where he had been slashed with a razor. The tip of the little finger on his left hand was missing: he'd been helping to lift a four-hundredweight safe when it had got out of control and crashed back on to his hand. That injury had cost him three years. The police had not had to be geniuses to know what to look for and they had asked all hospitals and doctors to report treatment of any man with a badly smashed finger. The Law had collected him and carried him off. The Law were bastards, but at least they weren't sanctimonious into the bargain. They never tried to reform him, which was what the rest of the world was always after doing.

Haggard climbed the shallow bank and stood on the grass ledge between the bank and the tall, overgrown hedge. From there, the armoured van would be clearly visible as it turned off the other road.

At the end of the lane was the disused and deserted brick factory. There, in one week's time, they would earn themselves thirty thousand.

He went down the slope, returned to the car, and drove up the lane to the brick factory. When he was backing round, he hit a pile of bricks that had been hidden by some tall grass. He cursed. The car was very precious.

2

FRINDHURST, on the south coast, had a population of just under 230,000. There was some industry, a summer trade in visitors, and a small port which handled coastal traffic and an ever-growing amount of pleasure boating.

The Frindhurst borough police force, established in 1910, had a strength of 460 officers and men. As in almost every other town in the world, the crime rate was rising and the percentage of crimes cleared up was falling, even though the Frindhurst police boasted a better clear-up rate, fifty-two per cent, than most other forces. Each year, the chief constable asked for a greater authorised strength, more vehicles, better communication systems including portable W/T sets for patrolling constables, and civilian staff to take over much of the clerical work: sometimes the Watch Committee refused to pass the requests, more often they passed them and it was the Finance Committee who squashed them. Frindhurst was no different in this respect from any other borough or county.

Every Monday morning, the chief constable, Charles Radamski, reported to the chairman of the Watch Committee, Reginald Breen. Neither man would ever have used the word 'report'. Radamski, as English as his well-dressed, stiffly upright figure and carefully trimmed moustache suggested, despite his name, earned £4,250 a year. He was satisfied with such a salary and intended to make certain it was his until he retired. One way of doing this was to keep on the right side of Breen. Breen ruled the Watch Committee and his more vocal detractors swore that if he told them to lie down on the floor and howl like dogs, they'd do it—in unison, at that.

The chief constable's black Austin Westminster turned off the road into the circular drive of Praemoor House, Breen's home. It stopped in front of the heavily pillared porch that might have proportionately suited a large country house, but certainly did not suit this square, chunky, red-brick house. The driver, a uniformed constable, climbed out and opened the rear door for Radamski.

'Thank you, Younger.' Radamski stepped clear of the car. 'Two-thirty, sharp?'

'Very good, sir.'

Radamski crossed to the porch. His lean, upright figure, his clipped speech, his excessive neatness, all contributed to the picture of a soldier turned policeman. He wore four World War II medals on his uniform, marking service in France and the Far East.

Very soon after ringing the chiming bell, the door was opened by a young woman with heavy, but attractive, features.

'Good morning, sir,' she said, and smiled. Her voice was heavily accented. 'It's a lovely day.'

'Hullo, Eva, how are you?'

'I am very well, thank you.' She drew in a deep breath before saying 'very' as she found it a word of almost insuperable difficulty.

She showed him into the large drawing-room, furnished with deliberate smartness. Breen and his wife were there.

'Hullo, Charles,' said Breen. 'It's good of you to come along.' Breen was always very careful to thank Radamski for coming along.

'Good morning, Vera, good morning, Reginald,' replied Radamski.

Vera Breen smiled warmly. She liked Radamski for his kindly good manners and for bringing her flowers from time to time. At fifty-two, age had not left her with much natural charm and few handsome men ever gave her flowers now. She was able never to wonder whether he would have done so had he not been chief constable and her husband chairman of the Watch Committee.

'Come and sit down, Charles. What will you drink? Gin,

whisky, Cinzano, or a *pineau des charentes* which I've just got hold of?'

'Might I have a whisky and soda?'

'The old favourite, eh? Not too much soda, isn't it?'

'And not too much whisky,' replied Radamski, automatically. 'I've rather a lot of work on hand.'

'I've never known you when you haven't, which is about the highest recommendation I can give any man.' Breen crossed to the cocktail cabinet, next to the glass-fronted cabinet in which was his wife's collection of Wedgwood Jasperware. He poured out two whiskies and a gin and Cinzano, then handed the glasses round.

'Cheers,' he said, 'and here's to the smartest police force in the south of England, and the north as well, come to that.'

Radamski smiled, showing just the right amount of modesty.

Breen stood with his back to the empty fireplace, in the grate of which were silver and gold painted pine cones. He was not a tall man, but people who met him were often inclined afterwards to think of him as tall. Born in Frindhurst, he had inherited one fairly successful furniture shop in the High Street when his father died. Now, at fifty-five, he was chairman and managing director of a company that owned seventeen large furniture shops, thirty-three smaller ones which catered for lower incomes, and a flourishing furniture factory. He was a clever man who managed never to appear clever.

Vera Breen said she must go to the kitchen and check that everything was in order for lunch and she went out, leaving her half empty glass of gin and Cinzano on the walnut pie-crust table.

'Are you smoking, Charles?' asked Breen, as the door closed behind his wife. He offered cigarettes. 'Well, how are things at the moment?'

'Not too bad. We've caught the boys who were committing that hooliganism in the parks.'

'That's good news. Considering all the money that's spent on the parks, it really was getting beyond a joke. Who are the boys?'

'Four teenagers from South Frindhurst, schoolboys with nothing better to do and all the time in the world to do it.'

'I suppose I'm hopelessly old-fashioned, but I just can't begin to understand this sort of thing.' Breen sat down in one of the leather arm-chairs. 'The lads today have everything and yet they go out of their way to cause malicious and senseless damage. Why is it, Charles? In the old days, lads were hungry and their fathers were on the dole and so they stole to try and feed themselves, but it was never much more than that. But now, when they've everything, they go out of their way to cause senseless damage.'

'It seems to be symptomatic of the age, but I'm damned if I know why. It's something more than just an initial lack of discipline, but I can't make out what.'

'I suppose we're just out of touch.' Breen shrugged his shoulders. 'Any serious crime?'

'Attempted rape at Postley, three thousand pounds' worth of jewellery stolen from a house two roads from here, and a breaking and entering in the High Street. Apart from them, just the routine incidents.'

Breen finished his drink. 'Which court will the boys appear in?'

'The Central Juvenile.'

'Old Glazer will be chairman, then. I'll have a word with him. The worst thing would be to let the boys off too lightly.' Breen stood up. He was a man who was seldom still for very long. 'How about the other half, Charles? There's time before lunch.'

'Thanks very much.'

Breen refilled their glasses.

'The two detectives from Regional Crime Squad joined this morning,' said Radamski.

Breen handed Radamski his glass and then took up position in front of the fireplace once more. 'What kind of men are they?'

'I haven't met them yet, but my D.C.I. says that the detective sergeant's a very old hand.'

Breen shook his head. 'It's a blasted nuisance. I've been against regional crime squads from the time they were first mooted.'

'I told them at that conference how we all felt about the idea.'

'They should have listened to you.'

'They did, but only with one ear. The Home Secretary's message to the conference was too much for them. His spokesman kept on and on about this being the age of motorways and internal air transport so that detectives must have the right to cross county and borough boundaries wherever and whenever necessary in order to keep up with the criminals.'

'It's just too easy to talk like that. It can be made to sound so simple: the criminal crosses a boundary, so the detectives are allowed to do the same and *ipso facto* the criminal is caught. But mark my words, nothing's going to be that easy and in any case there's excellent co-operation now between forces so that it's ridiculous to suppose a criminal's reached sanctuary the moment he crosses a border. All that talk is so much eyewash. The real stake here is as clear as a pikestaff: it's the independence of the various police forces. That's what the Home Secretary's determined to destroy. This country has always fought against a national police force and please God it always will. The government wants a national force because then it's got the perfect weapon for totalitarian purposes: look at what Goering and that crowd did in Germany. The moment he came to power, he dismissed all the police chiefs who didn't agree with his party's politics. That was the effective end of democracy.'

'So many of the other chief constables didn't seem to be able to see beyond the ends of their noses.'

'Frindhurst is a borough by Royal Charter, Charles, with its own police force of which anyone can be really proud. It's damned efficient and we're not going to give it up to those faceless politicians. My father always said that the day this town really developed a corporate spirit was the day its own police force came into being and the first contingent paraded down the High Street to the Mayor's reception. I'm not a lover of tradition for tradition's sake, but, by God, I'll fight like hell to keep this town's identity.'

Radamski sipped his whisky. The disappearance of the Frindhurst police force, within the next few years, would mean many things, including the loss of his job.

Vera Breen returned to the room. 'Lunch is ready. It's cold salmon, Charles. I do hope you like it?'

'Nothing more so.'

'That's wonderful.' She looked at her husband. 'I hope you haven't been getting all angry so that you won't enjoy the meal, Reggie?'

'I can't think about the nationalisation of the police without boiling, but I'm still damned hungry.'

. . . . .

Detective Chief Inspector Barnard looked round the room in the central police station which the two members of R.C.S. were to use. It was very barely furnished, having only two desks, a large wooden table with badly scarred top, and two grey filing cabinets. He spoke to the elder of the two men present. 'Are you settling in all right?'

'Yes, thank you, sir.'

'Have you got all you want?'

'We haven't a telephone yet, sir.'

'I'm afraid that'll take time.' Barnard looked round the room once more. 'You'll report to me regularly,' he said. He turned and left.

After the door was shut, Detective Sergeant Miller sat down on the edge of the nearer desk. 'A chummy lot, aren't they? Fair gushing goodwill.'

'We're new boys, strictly on probation,' replied Detective Constable Craig.

'If they don't want us, I'm more than willing to go back to county H.Q., even if this is supposed to be the most invigorating town on the coast. Talking about that, did you notice that poster on the railway platform?'

'No.'

'Even at my advanced age, that was plenty invigorating. If that girl's bikini top didn't fall off a split second after the photo was taken, I don't know much about gravity.'

Craig lit a cigarette. This move, from county C.I.D. to the Regional Crime Squad, had been represented to him by his chief as promotion. At the moment, it was difficult to view it in that light. Still, if he could accept the rest of what his chief had said, in a year's time he could expect to be accepted for Bramshill House, the police college, and if he did well enough there there was every chance he would be chosen for one of the new university courses designed to provide the police force with graduates who, when they held the higher ranks as it was presumed they would, necessarily would have a broadened mind. He'd earlier mentioned this possibility to Dusty Miller and had been surprised by the scornful references to Hendon and teaching coppers to drink with crooked little fingers.

Miller looked at his watch. 'A couple of hours to opening time. Roll on two hours.'

'I wonder what the digs'll turn out to be like.'

'Like always. The smell of boiled cabbage, dirty wallpaper, and psalm twenty-three on the bedroom wall.'

'They told me we'd soon be in regular police accommodation.'

'Police housing officers are the biggest liars out. They'll tell you anything, just to shut you up.'

Craig smiled.

. . . . . .

At nine-thirty that evening, Miller and Craig met in the public bar of The Red Lion, a dingy pub with an interesting collection of small wooden and china casks from which spirits had once been sold at a penny and twopence a nip.

'Have a fag?' said Miller, as they walked up to the bar.

'Not at the moment, thanks. I've been smoking like a chimney.'

Miller lit a cigarette. The barman came along the counter and Miller ordered two half-pints of light ale and two packets of crisps. 'I've a passion for crisps, but when the Missus is around I'm not allowed to eat 'em because they're supposed to put on weight. A decent's pot's the sign of happiness, I always say. You've never seen a well-bellied bloke dying from misery.'

The barman served them. Miller opened his packet of crisps, unwrapped the salt and poured it over the crisps. 'If only no one else had invented these things I could've done and now I'd be a millionaire and not some weary policeman, moved willy-nilly to a town where the posters talk about slipping bikinis but all you actually see are old women looking like sacks of potatoes. Here, let's go and sit down at one of those tables.'

They chose the circular table by the side of the window.

Miller mopped the sweat from his face with a handkerchief. 'It's hot enough for hell to fry.' He ate several crisps. 'What are your digs like?'

'Not very bright,' answered Craig. 'And just to add to the pleasures, the landlady's an old cow.'

'I'm lucky, for once, but that won't be the fault of the housing officer.'

'I doubt he deliberately chooses lousy places.'

'You haven't been in the force long enough to know what he does deliberately.'

'You're obviously a very determined pessimist.'

'I've been a policeman long enough to have become a realist.'

Miller ate some more crisps as he thought about Craig. Craig could almost be called a misfit in the present-day force: he believed in a sense of vocation, he thought he was carrying out a public duty. With the kind of public that was around today, how in the hell could anyone believe they were owed a duty? They'd stand around any day of the week and watch a policeman being beaten up by thugs. The police found themselves nearer in spirit to the villains than to the public, who demanded law and order but refused the police

the powers necessary to keep either. In the old days, you belted
a juvenile delinquent a couple of hard ones and he wasn't a
juvenile delinquent any longer: do that today and you were
up in court. He'd have left the force a couple of years back
because the sense of frustration—and the hours of duty—
had become too great, but these extra years would average
out his pay to provide a better pension. That was the one
good thing to say for the modern force: there was a reasonable pension.

Unknowingly, Craig interrupted Miller's train of thoughts.
'When's the wife arriving?'

'Tomorrow, all being well. She had to stay back because of
the kids and clearing things up, but she's due in the late afternoon. Talking about the Missus, have some more crisps? This
time tomorrow, they'll be off the ration.'

Craig, to forestall Miller, hastily stood up and crossed to
the bar where he ordered two more beers and two more
packets of crisps.

Miller watched him as he stood by the bar. University
degrees! How many villains did they think a university degree
would catch? And what the hell was the use of the special
course at Bramshill, deliberately planned on county-house
lines? What did people want? Spit and polish, salutes, and
don't eat your dinner with your knife you might cut your
tongue? There was more than enough bull at the moment,
without going out of one's way to import more. Up at county
H.Q., a policeman still had to clean down the car belonging to
the chairman of the council. The chairman was a retired fish-
monger. Why couldn't he clean his own car: did it stink too
much of fish for his delicate nostrils?

Craig returned to the table and put down the glasses of beer
and two packets of crisps. 'You looked just then as if you was
suffering, Dusty.'

'I was, lad, I was. Thinking about the way the force is
degenerating.'

'A terrible bad entry coming in these days?'

'All right, you wait. You see what happens to your precious
law and order with all the men leaving the force.'

'They'll get better recruitment and less waste now they're putting up pay and cutting down overtime.'

'Cutting down overtime? You'll be a grandfather before that happens. Anyway, that's not the trouble. D'you want to know what is?'

'You obviously want to tell me.'

'It's the public. Deep down in their little hearts, they hate us. We're authority, and they hate authority until they need its assistance.'

'Twaddle. The last opinion poll . . .'

'Opinion poll? I wouldn't consult one of them to find out what happened last week. The public hates us. Look how they've gone out of their way to make our job impossible. What happens now? If we catch one of the real villains, the worst that happens to him is a little lecture and maybe a couple of years in prison. Flogging's out, P.D.'s soon going to be out, hanging's out . . .'

'Hanging never stopped anyone committing a murder.'

'It was pretty effective at stopping the hanged man from committing a second murder.'

'You know something, Dusty? You're one of those awful hidebound reactionaries our local Labour chap was talking about.'

'Jeer away, but I know my crooks and villains. There's only one way to keep a villain under and that's to slap the charge round his neck so hard it throttles him. And what's more, don't worry how you get round to slapping it.'

'That's hardly the advice they give in textbooks.'

'There's one good use for textbooks on fighting criminals, but that's not in any flaming classroom at precious Bramshill House.'

'Sergeant, you're trying to be a bad influence.'

'I'm trying to teach you the glimmerings of being a policeman.'

Craig wondered how much of Miller's talk was a leg-pull and how much expressed genuinely held beliefs. Miller was certainly of the old bash-and-break brigade, but he also had a keen, if bitter, sense of humour. Even a short acquaintance had shown that there was nothing he liked more than a rowdy argument which he would prolong by exaggerating his own beliefs to the point of distortion.

Miller drank half his second pint of beer. He opened one of the packets of crisps and spread the salt. 'In next to no time, it'll all be behind me. I'll be retired, digging potatoes and planting cabbages.'

'Have you decided where you're going to live?'

'We wouldn't mind somewhere round here in spite of all the old women, but we haven't a chance with the price of housing. The Missus was left a little bit by her father, but it wouldn't buy a couple of window-sills down here.'

'Housing's hell.'

'That's why it pays every time to join a borough force, even if promotion is slower than a tortoise. Buy a house on mortgage and enjoy yourself.' Miller finished his beer. 'Come on, lad, get thy stomach awash and thy kidneys working.'

'No more for me, thanks.'

'You're not finishing your first day's work with R.C.S. without drowning your sorrows in drink. Anyway, once you're married you'll realise it pays never to miss a chance. When my Missus is around, my beer intake'll go down towards zero.'

'That'll save money for the house.'

Miller chuckled. 'Some houses are too dearly bought.' He stood up and went over to the bar.

Craig thought about Daphne. As happened sometimes, he found it difficult to remember exactly what she looked like, which sounded ridiculous: but absence did create a shimmer in his memory. She wanted them to get married, but he was positive they should wait until he could be sure his future was as rosy as some people said it was. She was gay, vivacious, and passionate. So passionate, that she wasn't worried how far they went in their love-making. He was. As she said, that seemed a very topsyturvy way of things.

'Here we are,' said Miller, as he returned with two glasses and two packets of crisps. 'Have a coffin-stick now?'

Craig accepted one of the tipped cigarettes from the battered packet.

'I drink to crime,' said Miller, as he raised his glass in mock salute. 'It may not keep us in luxury, but at least it prevents us from starving.' He drank, and then opened his third packet of crisps and spread the salt.

3

HAGGARD studied his reflection in the mirror and fractionally straightened his tie. Looking smart was what a smart bloke did. Look smart and act a bit contemptuous and a jeweller would let you walk away with half a dozen diamond rings on appro.: dress like a tramp and he wouldn't let you come within ten feet of the door without blasting off the alarm bells.

Florence, sitting on the oval bed, spoke. 'I want to go out to dinner.'

He smoothed down the right coat lapel.

'I said I want to go out to dinner.'

He turned round. Florence was a brass, the smartest brass for miles. She claimed she could make a hundred quid a week on her turf and he believed her.

'Are you going to take me out?'

'No.'

'Suppose I find someone else to take me?'

'No one's holding you back.' He laughed at her and she called him a few obscene names. He'd always attracted women, ever since he'd known there were two different sexes. He treated them with contemptuous indifference, even antipathy, and only one had ever had the guts to try and stripe him. He wondered whether Flo would one day go for him: she got so jealous over him, she might do.

'Where are you going?' she demanded.

'To see my grandmother.'

She cursed his grandmother. She had beautiful auburn hair, a perfect oval face, and an ability to look totally pure and virtuous.

'I'm bored,' she said.
'Count your toes and see if you've got ten like other people.'
'Come here.'
He crossed to the bed. She lay back, careful to let her skirt slide up her legs. He lit a cigarette. She cursed him once more, sat up, smoothed her skirt down with a gesture of modesty. She stared angrily at the far wall.

He liked seeing a bird sweat. In the nick, especially when they'd shoved him in the chokey for some minor infringement of the rules, like belting a screw, he'd sit back and think of all the birds he'd known and how they'd crawled to him. Most men needed skirt so badly they did the crawling: they were soft. In this world, whenever two people met one had to crawl: a real man made certain he remained standing.

She could no longer remain silent. 'What are you thinking about, Tom?'

He grinned. 'I was thinking of making you crawl.'

'D'you want me to?' she asked eagerly.

'Forget the stunts. I was talking metaphorically.' That completely fooled her, as he'd known it would. He'd never had any proper education because he'd never been prepared to knock up his brains for some spineless schoolmaster, but he had a natural intelligence and a desire to learn. Quite often, he jeered at that desire. What was he after getting—like all those smart Ikeys in London who swindled everyone? He never knew the answer. He read a great deal. He liked books by authors who'd rejected the standards of the world and told the world where to jump: like D. H. Lawrence, who discovered four-letter words, and Karl Marx who discovered how to make the rich sweat.

She couldn't stand silence for very long. 'When will you be back?' she asked.

'When I reckon on it.'

'But what am I going to do?'

'See if any of your customers are free?'

'All right, I will,' she shouted.

He laughed. She knew what he'd do to her if he caught her with anyone else: she'd never again look young, pure, innocently fresh.

He left the room and the flat and crossed the landing to the lift. These were luxury flats and not all of them were let because a thousand pounds a year was a lot of rent. He could afford a thousand a year at the moment, and as to the future, who the hell knew anything about tomorrow? They might drop the Bomb and people would only be concerned about their plots in hell. If they did drop the Bomb, he hoped he'd die in debt and with a bird by his side: that was the way to die.

The lift took him down to the ground floor. He went out through the lobby to the forecourt, which was the car-park. His Buick looked like a whale amongst a shoal of minnows. A man had to have money to buy a car like that.

He drove to Soapy Brown's house and Brown's wife let him into the dirty, smelly hall. Brown seemed to like dirt as other men liked women.

Brown, Denton, and Grant were sitting in the front room, around the table, drinking whisky. They looked up with evident relief as he entered. Without him, they'd never get near the big league. He had power over them. One of the prison psychiatrists had said he was a natural leader and what a pity it was he hadn't gone into the army. He had, but seldom moved any further than the glasshouse. The army didn't want natural leaders: it wanted unthinking cannon-fodder, ready to die unthinkingly at the command of any dewy-eyed second-lieutenant.

Denton was the first to speak. 'How's the world?'

'Still turning.'

'Have a whisky?' Denton poured out a stiff whisky into a dirty glass and handed it to Haggard, who carefully cleaned the rim of the glass. Denton had been a con man and he still often talked and acted the part.

Conversation became general. Haggard noticed that Brown was talking very quickly and not listening to anyone. He was nervous. Haggard hated nervous people because you never knew when their nerve would give out, but there wasn't another torch-artist of equal calibre this side of Scotland. Give Soapy Brown an oxy-acetylene burner and he'd all but play tunes with the thing.

Haggard took a packet of Camels from his pocket and offered it around. The cigarettes had his monogram on them. That really tickled him. He sat down on the edge of the table. 'Have you got the burner, Soapy?'

'It's all laid on.'

'And plenty of bottles of gas?'

'Enough to cut the van in two.'

Haggard spoke to Denton. 'What abut the light van?'

'I picked one up at the back of Piccadilly. The number plate's all changed and it's ready.'

'And the car?'

'A three point eight Jag, nearly new,' said Grant.

'Where d'you get it?'

'Like we said, Brighton.'

'Changed the plates?'

'Yes.'

'Have you got the uniform?'

'It's all safe and sound,' said Brown eagerly. 'Everything's ready, just everything.'

Haggard ignored the assurance. 'The dope?'

'That's ready.'

'Have you tried the tins?'

'I tried each one and they near made me sick.'

'Signs?'

'They're next door,' said Grant. 'One road up and three diversions and spares.'

Haggard nodded. Grant was a man like himself, a professional who'd learned the hard way that you couldn't plan too carefully. Some of the old hands laughed at detailed planning, but they did most of their laughing in the nick.

'What happens if they ignore the notices?' asked Denton.

'We're dead unlucky, aren't we?' Haggard spoke with open contempt. Carried through the gates of Paradise, Denton would ask what would happen if they crumbled on to him. Haggard spoke to Grant. 'How's the wireless equipment, Ringo?'

'Ready.'

Haggard always found it vaguely astonishing that Grant had once been a wireless operator in the Merchant Navy. He'd stayed at sea until a customs officer found two thousand quid's worth of undeclared watches in his possession. After the sixth whisky, Grant was eager to tell how that customs man had pocketed the two hundred quid bribe and then run him in for smuggling. When they counted the watches, there were twenty missing. The customs man knew a couple of opportunities when he saw them.

Haggard held out his glass for it to be refilled. 'Have you all got the times?'

They said they had. Brown poured himself out his fourth whisky. He was scared of Haggard and needed something to counter that fear. He'd started working back in the days when violence was unusual, but the new generation treated it as an essential part of villaining. You didn't have to know much about Haggard to sense that whenever violence would help, he'd use it.

'You start the jammer half-way along Brooklyn Road,' said Haggard to Grant. 'Should anything go wrong, get ahead of the armoured van and pick up Bill.'

'Nothing's going to go wrong with my end of things.'

Haggard smiled, showing his white even teeth.

* * * * *

On Friday morning, at nine-thirty-five, a post office engineer fixed the telephone in the R.C.S. room at Frindhurst central police station. After the engineer had gone, Miller said that when one's superiors had a direct line of communication, they had an annoying habit of using it. For once, his expressed pessimism was justified. At ten-thirty the detective inspector at county H.Q. rang up to report a series of petty swindles from jewellers in neighbouring counties and to say that the assistant chief constable, in operational control of the district committee, would be making a tour of inspection in the near future, probably in company with an Inspector of Constabulary. He went on to express the hope that Frindhurst R.C.S control would be in full and working order.

Miller swore as he replaced the receiver and looked across at the second desk where Craig was filing the latest list of index numbers of stolen cars. 'The silver-caps are coming out on a conducted tour of inspection.'

'When?'

'Could be any time, so before tonight stuff some papers into the drawers of the filing cabinets, hang a couple of lists of something on the walls, and put a couple of folders on top of each desk. In the meantime, go along to the D.C.I. and tell him there's a rash of petty larcenies by substitution from jewellers in Kent and Essex. H.Q. wants all jewellers in the area warned. Bloke's twenty to twenty-five, brown wavy hair, long face, and speaks with a Kensington accent.'

Craig left the room and went down the main stairs to the detective chief inspector's room. Barnard accepted the report and said rather sourly that he didn't see why it took anyone from R.C.S. to handle such a trifling matter.

Craig got a list of jewellers from the duty sergeant and went out and along to Quarrington Street. Here were most of the banks, solicitors, and estate agents. Robbers' Lane, the locals called it. A patrolling constable exchanged a few words with him, and as he continued walking he reflected that the rank and file of the Frindhurst police force were friendly, whatever the senior officers might be. He stopped outside a jeweller's and stared at two trays of engagement rings in the window. There was only one ring there attractive enough for Daphne and it cost forty-five pounds. It was a hell of a lot of money. He went inside and tried to warn the middle-aged jeweller against being robbed, but the jeweller said no one would ever succeed in tricking him.

Craig returned to the pavement and looked at his watch. Ten-fifty-eight. The sunshine covered the west side of the road and brought a sparkle to the shops and offices. He noticed a blonde in a silk blouse with a plunging neckline. Daphne had once worn a neckline like that, only less so: he'd kicked up such a fuss she never wore that dress again. He was damned if he was going to share his pleasures. He watched the blonde walk along the pavement, bottom waggling. It was a nice, quiet, drowsy morning, the kind of morning when one could take time off in which to appreciate the beauties of nature.

4

THE armoured van drew up before the bank. The driver switched off the engine. He checked that the alarm system was ready, then climbed out of the cab and went round to the rear doors, which he unlocked. He heard the rasping noise as the interior bolts were withdrawn and he pulled open the right-hand door.

The Alsatian came forward to the edge of the compartment and sniffed him. He backed away slightly. Everyone knew that, no matter how well trained, an Alsatian could turn vicious in a second.

The three guards jumped down on to the road. They drew a slightly higher rate of pay than the driver and the guard who sat in the cab because of the discomfort of riding in the back where there were no windows and precious little ventilation. This differential was a constant source of annoyance.

The driver stayed by the armoured van as the four other guards and the Alsatian went into the bank.

Inside the bank, the first teller signalled to the guards to come to his counter. He was handed the requisition note which was written confirmation of the figure given to the bank the previous day by telephone. Three steel cases were put on the counter.

The teller carried two of the cases to the rear and through one of the far doors. A girl, who had been working an adding machine, left her seat and came to pick up the third bag. The youngest of the guards smiled at her, but she ignored the greeting. The Alsatian, lead unclipped, sat at the feet of the handler.

The teller returned with two cases, which he put on the counter, and the girl brought the third one. 'Who's signing today?' he asked.

The nearest man said he would and took the paper from the teller and scrawled his signature at the bottom.

The guards fixed the waist chains to the cases. The eldest man visually checked they were ready and led the way outside.

They went through the swing doors and out on to the pavement. Automatically, two men looked right and two looked left. A couple of women went past, talking loudly: a small boy watched them with excited interest: a dog seemed about to challenge the Alsatian, but finally decided against this.

The driver was standing by the open rear doors of the armoured van. The three guards carrying the cases of money climbed inside, the Alsatian jumped in, and the driver shut the doors and locked them. He heard the inner bolts slide home. He went round to the cab and climbed in behind the wheel. The fourth guard was already in the other seat.

Inside the cargo compartment, the overhead light was just strong enough for the men to be able to see each other reasonably clearly. Since they could not smoke, because the ventilation was so poor, they sat morosely on the hard seats and waited for the van to complete its journey, whereupon they would return to another bank and draw another large sum of money for another factory's pay roll. It was a dull, boring life.

In a near-by parking bay, Ringo Grant switched on the engine of the Jaguar. He wanted to smoke, but could not. Haggard was smart and it was he who had forbidden them to carry anything at all in their pockets, which meant no smoking until the job was done because the dried spit on a cigarette stub could tell the splits the blood group of the smoker. Haggard was smart enough not to give the splits as much as the time of day.

Grant took his gloved hands off the steering-wheel and turned them over so that he could check once again that the palms and finger-tips of the gloves were undamaged. No villain intelligent enough to sign his own name left direct finger-prints around in the present day and age, but it was incredible how many worked with damaged gloves and deposited part of a print. The splits didn't need much of a print to begin to get to work.

The armoured van drew out from the kerb and joined the thin stream of traffic. Grant let two cars go past before he left the parking bay. There was the tight, sick feeling of excitement and nervousness within him that always came when a job was actually on. He momentarily wondered whether Haggard ever suffered such sensation.

The armoured van passed the lights at green. The car immediately ahead of Grant was turning right and it slowed down to a halt to wait for traffic coming in the opposite direction. Grant cursed. The lights changed to red. The car ahead turned right as the road cleared and Grant drove on, under the bows of a lorry coming from the right.

The armoured van slowed to go round the island and into Quarrington Road, the following car went round the island and carried along the High Street, and now the Jaguar was immediately behind the van.

Grant stared at the back doors of the van. Behind them was thirty thousand quid. Six thousand for each man in the team, provided expenses hadn't run too high. Six thousand to spend on living and no need to worry about tomorrow because Haggard had said they'd work as a team from now on. They'd be a first-class team. Haggard was clever enough to know just how to plan: planning on the scale that had gone into the present job meant that there wasn't a chance of failure.

As the Jaguar turned left into Station Road and went over the railway bridge, Grant looked down quickly at the passenger seat. On the seat was the electronic jammer, inside an ordinary portable wireless case for camouflage. This would prevent any effective wireless transmission from the van. He'd been a bit of a genius with that jammer. There'd be no message from the van received to give a change of course or an alarm.

As the Jaguar passed the large garage with dozens of used cars for sale on the oblong forecourt, Grant switched on the jammer and the car's wireless set. The wireless gave out a hideous cacophony of wailing static.

His hands and neck were beaded with sweat and the churning feeling in his stomach was stronger.

Three quarters of a mile away, at the T-junction which marked the end of Brooklyn Road, Denton climbed into the Mini and drove on. He left behind him two signs on the left-hand side of the road. One was in black and white and said 'Police Notice. Road Up', the other was in yellow and black and said 'A.A. Diversion' with an arrow indicating the direction for cars to take.

Denton drove very quickly, so quickly that when he reached the right-hand bend he had to brake sharply. He forced himself to calm down. Being introspective, he once again asked himself how much of a coward he really was. In the old days, when he had gone in for confidence tricks, there had been little fear of physical trouble, but here, if the slightest thing went wrong . . .

He abruptly realised he had reached the right-hand turn and he braked to a halt. He put out a second A.A. diversion sign with the arrow pointing to the road on the right. An oncoming car obediently turned. Denton thought how right Haggard had been. Tell the world to jump and, without thought, it jumped.

He turned into the right-hand road and then right again into the lane with the 'No Through Road' sign. A little along the lane was a small natural lay-by where the grass verge temporarily broadened out. He parked the car and picked up from the rear seat another diversion sign and an empty half-hundredweight paper sack.

He climbed up the bank and stood in the cover of the overgrown blackthorn hedge. Just as Grant had wanted to smoke, he had a terrible desire to do so.

He saw the van as it came along the other road. There was no other vehicle in front of it and only the Jaguar behind it. He ran down the slope, posted the A.A. diversion sign with the arrow pointing into the small lane, and covered the 'No Through Road' sign with the paper sack. He ran back up the slope and knelt down.

The van and then the Jaguar passed him. He ran back down the slope, kicked over the diversion sign on to its face, and jerked the paper sack off the 'No Through Road' sign. He heard a car approach and turned his back on it. The car went past the lane.

Along the lane, the driver of the armoured van cursed. His vehicle was a large one and the narrow lane seemed to be getting more and more twisty.

The van turned a last corner and came in sight of the deserted office buildings, the oblong kilns with rusted corrugated iron roofs, and the tall brick stacks, one of which had collapsed. Beyond all the buildings were the water filled pits which marked the clay diggings.

'Some diversion,' muttered the driver, as he braked to a stop.

The second man in the cab shrugged his shoulders, switched on the wireless transmitter, and reported that unit Arthur Barker six was lost, thanks to the fools who put up the road signs. He switched over in order to receive confirmation of his message, but only a stream of ear-splitting static came out of the loudspeaker.

The driver looked in his rear-view mirror. A Jaguar had drawn up behind. He was glad he was not the only one to be made a fool of.

A policeman came in sight. His peaked cap was pulled down well over his forehead and he sported a bushy moustache. He came up to the driver's side of the cab.

'What the hell's going on?' shouted the driver.

The policeman shook his head to show he could not hear and tried the door handle. The driver released the inside catch and himself pushed open the door.

'What nit put out them diversion signs . . .?' he began.

Haggard reached in, grabbed hold of the driver by his coat, and pulled him out. The driver tried to save himself, but he fell to the ground awkwardly and a fierce stab of pain hit his shoulder.

Brown, face covered by a nylon stocking, ran up to the armoured van with the fibreglass baffler in his right hand. Grant, face also covered, was already out of the Jaguar and standing by the side of the van. He held his hands together to give Brown a foothold. Brown stepped on to his hands and Grant, sweating from the effort, raised him up. Brown dropped the baffler over the small grill on the top of the roof. So complete was the surprise of the attack that it was several seconds after the baffler was in place that the alarm was sounded. The baffler reduced the noise to one that could not be heard at any distance.

Haggard twice slammed the lead filled cosh down on the driver's head and knocked him unconscious. Haggard turned his back to the van, removed his cap, and pulled a nylon stocking over his head. When he looked back, he saw that Denton and Brown were struggling with the second guard. They had dragged him out of the cab, but he was a powerful man who knew how to defend himself and was throwing short punches that were hurting them.

'Use your canes,' shouted Haggard, almost incoherent because of anger. They had coshes and should have finished the job long ago, but each man seemed reluctant to use one. What a time to go soft!

Haggard ran forward and slammed his cosh down on the guard's neck. Incredibly, the man seemed unaffected by the blow and he brought up his truncheon and pressed the release button on it. A stream of liquid squirted out with sufficient force to pierce the nylon stockings. Denton cried out once from the agony and reeled away, frantically rubbing his eyes through the stocking.

Haggard landed a second blow, a third one, and then a fourth one. He felt a violent need to smash this man who was threatening to ruin everything. The guard had fallen to his knees. The skin was split above his right ear and blood was spilling down the side of his face. Haggard used his cosh twice more. The guard collapsed in an untidy heap. Haggard kicked the man's head and then buried his shoe in the other's guts. The bastard had nearly ruined everything. The stupid bastard.

Grant was holding a large aerosol can up to the ventilator grill, high up on the right-hand side of the van. He pressed the release knob and gas hissed between the slats of the ventilator into the interior. He turned to see how the fight was going and inadvertently moved his right hand sufficiently to direct the nozzle away from the grill. The spray, half liquid, half gas, hit the side of the van and was directed back at him. It made him cough violently.

From inside the van came continuous coughing and frenzied shouting. Someone hammered on the side with his fists. Grant remembered reading about the way in which the inmates of Auschwitz had been gassed and he shuddered. But he kept the release button depressed. The hammering on the side of the van went on. The aerosol container emptied and he chucked it down on to the ground and picked up the second full one. As he removed the safety cover over the release button, the hammering suddenly stopped and he thought he heard the sounds of a man collapsing to the floor. Haggard had said to use up both containers even though that would make the concentration of gas inside dangerous to life. Even while he was horrified by what he was doing, Grant aimed the second container at the grill and pressed the release button. He hoped to God none of them inside was sufficiently conscious to be able to start hammering again.

Brown had gone round to the far side of one of the buildings. He came back, driving the van stolen from Piccadilly. He braked it to a halt a few feet from the armoured van and then he and Haggard unloaded the oxy-acetylene equipment. Denton was kneeling, still trying to ease some of the pain from his eyes.

When the second tin of gas was empty, Grant dropped it and ran back to the Jaguar. He reversed the car, turned, and drove back to the rusting gates. He left the car there and took up position as look-out on the bank of the lane. It was unlikely anyone would come up the lane, but if so he would give the alarm. As he settled down, he kept hearing the hammering there had been.

Back at the armoured van, Brown connected up the burner to the bottles of gas. This burner would cut through anything but the side of a battleship, but it used up oxygen at the rate of ten thousand gallons an hour which was why they had had to bring such a large supply with them. He put on protective helmet with dark blue visor and climbed into the cab of the armoured van, rubber pipes trailing after him. He lit the burner and the roaring flame quickly changed from yellow to an icy blue.

He aimed the flame at a point in the bulkhead eighteen inches above the passenger seat. The uncomfortable working position made his muscles ache and the heat made him sweat profusely, but these worries were submerged in the almost overwhelming fear of what would happen when the flame pierced the metal so that the gas inside was free to escape. Haggard had sworn that not enough would come out to worry a fieldmouse, but Brown had had nightmares in which it reached out to dive down into his lungs and torment them as his father's lungs had been tormented when he tried to gas himself twenty-two years before.

Only Brown worked. Haggard stood close to the two unconscious men, laid side by side, and stared at the cab of the armoured van: Denton had removed the stocking from his head and was rubbing his eyes with a handkerchief: Grant maintained his watch from the bank above the lane.

After eight minutes, Brown had cut almost a complete circle out of the bulkhead, leaving only enough metal to hold the inner disc in position. He turned off the burner and climbed out of the cab, moving stiffly because of his muscles.

Haggard walked across.

'It's all ready,' said Brown.

Haggard pushed past and climbed into the cab. He knocked out the inner disc with clenched fist and shone a torch into the interior. The three men were lying in crumpled-up, fetal positions and the Alsatian was on its side with all four legs out stiff. 'O.K.,' he shouted.

Brown returned with a fan that had a long lead. They fixed the fan in the cab so that it would extract the air from inside the compartment and connected the lead to the van's battery. As soon as the fan was working, Haggard checked that both doors were fully open and he smashed the windscreen.

When Brown was ordered back to resume burning, he swore the stink of gas was too strong. Haggard hustled him into the cab with brutal force and, even more frightened of Haggard than of the gas, Brown resumed work. He cut out a hole that stretched from the top of the seat to the roof.

Once the gear was out of the cab, Haggard took a deep breath and wriggled through the hole into the rear compartment. He reached the back doors by the light of the torch and withdrew the two heavy bolts. The doors had been unlocked on the outside by Brown, who had taken the keys from the unconscious driver's pocket, and when Haggard kicked them, they opened. He dropped to the ground and thankfully drew fresh air into his lungs.

They dragged the men to the rear of the compartment and cut the chains which held the three metal money cases. It was obvious that the dog was dead and from the look of the guards they also could have been dying.

The cases were locked. Brown began to try to force the lock of one of them, but stopped the moment Haggard shouted at him to rush them to the Jaguar. Brown might, thought Haggard with wild anger, be a torch artist, but he'd been on holiday when they handed out intelligence.

Haggard watched the three cases carried over to the boot of the Jaguar. He looked round. The rear door of the armoured van was open and the sunlight picked out the bodies of two guards and the feet of the third. The gas had cost fifty quid a tin, but even at that it had been cheap. Three guards and a guard dog who were out of the fight before they ever entered it. He turned and studied the two guards lying in the dust. The driver seemed to be twitching slightly, but he wasn't going to be up and around for a hell of a time yet. The other man was lying inert and the dust around his chin had been turned into mud by his blood. The stupid bastard. Trying to imitate a hero. What the hell was he after, a framed vote of thanks? It wasn't his money that was being pinched, so what if he lost it?

Haggard walked across to the van in which they'd carried the oxy-acetylene equipment. He checked it inside and out and was satisfied that a dozen detective superintendents could crawl all over it day and night for a week and still not find the smell of a clue.

He changed out of the uniform into a suit and walked towards the Jaguar. It had been four men against five and the four had won, hands down.

Denton, Grant, and Brown were by the car. They stared at him. 'Why didn't you hit the bastard?' he said to Denton.

Denton, eyes red from the spray and his rubbing, made no reply.

'All right. Get moving.'

Haggard, Denton, and Brown climbed into the Jaguar, Grant went along the lane to the Mini.

They drove out on to the road. Haggard accelerated fiercely, soon leaving the Mini behind. He prided himself on being a superb driver: in the class of Nouvolari and Moss. If there were someone in the world he admired, and envied, even regarded with a trace of awe, it was either of those two. They were men with fire in their guts, dependent on no one, fighting the world and death. The speedometer of the Jaguar showed seventy-five as they rounded a shallow bend.

They reached Gresham at twelve-thirty-one and drove through the heavy traffic of market day. Beyond the railway station were two parking areas, belonging to the railway, one in the forecourt of the station and the other a quarter of a mile up the road. Strangely, the second one was never more than half full.

Haggard parked the Jaguar alongside an old 20/25 Rolls-Royce. Two cars beyond that was his yellow Buick. He climbed out, took off his gloves, and stuffed them into his trouser pocket. He went round to the back of the Jaguar and opened the boot. He remembered how the others had been terrified by the idea of transferring the cases from the Jaguar to the Buick in the middle of a public car-park, but then there were things they'd never understand, not if they grew beards down to their toes: wasn't it G. K. Chesterton who wrote about the postman no one saw because, as a postman, he became to others merely part of the scenery? If they'd transferred the cases from car to car in some remote country lane it would have been ten to one that some half-witted yokel was around to watch: but transfer them in the middle of a public car-park and there could be a multitude of people around and no one would notice a thing.

They carried the three cases from the Jaguar to the Buick. Haggard stared at them, in the boot, and once again knew the sharp mental uplift of success. He'd beaten five guards, an Alsatian, a 'fool-proof' system, and a 'thief-proof' armoured van. If they handed out marks for robberies, he'd have a full score. He slammed the boot lid shut, locked it, and went round towards the driving door. As he swerved slightly, to prevent his trousers catching on the edge of the rear bumper, one of the gloves dropped out of his pocket. He did not notice this.

Just before he sat in the driving seat, he saw the expressions on Brown's and Denton's faces. They were frightened and were desperately wishing him to get moving. He brought out a packet of cigarettes from one of the cubby-holes and wasted a lot of time in lighting a cigarette. The job they had just done sorted out the men from the boys.

They drove the seventeen miles from Gresham to Telton and stopped outside Brown's house. Grant came out and carried one of the cases inside.

When, later, Haggard left the house, he was carrying two fibreglass suitcases in which were £15,038—£6,000 was for The Lip, who'd come up with all the right answers; £3,000 was for expenses, and of this almost £1,000 would be clear profit for him since he had claimed a figure far in excess of what the expenses had really been; £6,038 was his share of what remained.

He put the two cases in the boot of the Buick and then went round to the driving seat. He started the engine, but did not immediately drive off. Seven thousand pounds. A man could live for a bit on that. A man could flash the cabbage around and play the horses or try the roulette wheel. A man could drop a couple of one-ers in an evening's play and still walk out, smiling, which was more than all your respectable rat-racers could do.

He drove across Telton to the flat and parked the Buick next to a Rapier. These were luxury flats, but he was the only tenant with a truly luxury car. That must make some of the others sick. He picked up the suitcases from the boot and carried them into the building.

Florence, not trying to hide her nervousness, was waiting for him. She was dressed in a simple blouse and skirt and had been constantly fidgeting with the blouse so that it was at one point badly creased. When she saw him, she relaxed.

She came over and kissed him. He pressed his hands in the small of her back and then arched her backwards. She tried to ignore the pain, but it very soon became too great. She begged him to stop and when he didn't she clawed his face. He laughed and released her. They went into the bedroom and undressed. A successful job always made him feel randy.

Because one of the gloves had already fallen out of his trouser pocket, there was not much of a bulge to mark the remaining one. He forgot it.

5

CRAIG looked out of the window of the R.C.S. room in Frindhurst central police station. Beyond, all was warmth and sunshine. He yawned.

'What's the matter?' asked Miller. 'Overworked?'

'And underpaid.'

'Write a letter to the silver-hats. They're very interested in the thoughts of underpaid coppers.'

Craig was no longer surprised by Miller's attitude to Authority, nor did he believe the other ever joked when he discussed the subject. Part of Miller's mind was almost completely inflexible, with everything in strictly delineated compartments, which almost certainly was one of the reasons why he'd been lucky even to gain promotion to detective sergeant. To Miller, Authority was something to be knocked at every opportunity. It was the old sweat's cry of kill off the generals. What was entertaining was the fact that Miller never apparently began to recognise how exactly his attitude mirrored the one which so aroused his scorn: he was always trying to turn the clock back, to the time when a great deal of justice was dispensed by the copper on the beat.

'When's your leave coming up?' asked Miller, after a pause.

'The D.I. at H.Q. said I could scratch some just as soon as we settled in here.'

'Pigs might fly.'

Craig was inclined to agree with that pessimistic outlook. Police leave was one of those things which always looked all right on paper, but rarely survived intact the transition from paper to fact.

The telephone rang. Miller lifted the receiver, listened for several seconds, thanked the caller, and replaced the receiver. 'A security van is overdue with thirty thousand quid which it picked up in the High Street half an hour ago.'

'And no word from anyone since?'

'Apparently not.'

'Then it must have been lifted?'

Miller leaned back in his chair. 'Thirty thousand quid. What couldn't a man do with that? Me and the Missus could live in the Canary Islands like we've always wanted to.'

'What a hope! I've yet to hear of a policeman who retires rich.'

Miller shrugged his shoulders. One or two policemen, mercifully no more, retired with more money than they ever earned. He'd even known one of them. But Craig would never believe a policeman could dishonour his uniform. Craig was a nice, friendly bloke who'd been a police cadet and over four years in the force apparently without ever having got his nose down to the stink. Maybe that was why they were talking of sending him to Bramshill and the university afterwards. The modern line of thought was soft enough to believe that a degree was the best weapon to fight the villains with.

* * * * *

Radamski's room at the central police station was large, light and airy, and fitted out with very comfortable, almost luxurious, furniture.

He sat at his desk and stared at the photographic portrait of his wife. She was still a beautiful woman. Life had been kind and had given him a happy marriage, two healthy children, and for some time now a good job which exactly suited him. After the last war, he had tried to stay in the army because the regimental life greatly appealed to him, but his application for a permanent commission had failed. For a short while it had seemed he was destined to be a square peg in a succession of ever rounder holes, then the old-boy network had come to his assistance and gained for him a chief constableship in the days before the Home Secretary had been given the right to veto any such appointment from outside the service. He'd become chief constable to a small and inefficient borough force: by the time he left for his present job, the force had become efficient, with a high morale.

Now, he held one of the more lucrative chief constableships and was paid an annual salary of £4,250. For that, he had to run the police force to the best of his ability, which he did, and it was not boasting to say it was run damned well, and to learn to work with Reginald Breen. Breen knew what he wanted and how to get it, always in the name of some democratically conceived committee, but in him there ran no wish to play the part of a dictator, enjoying power for power's sake. All his actions were born of a deep love and respect for his home town. He was certain he knew what was best for Frindhurst and the people who lived there and since he had a finger in any number of pies, he was able to see that the town got what he believed it should. Strangely, he was far more often right than wrong.

Radamski thought about Breen's reactions to the Regional Crime Squad. A lot of people shouted loudly about how much more efficient regional forces were going to make crime detection in the country, even if this was inevitably the first step towards a national police force. But could one be quite so complacent about such an outcome—wasn't Breen right to point out warningly to the example of Goering and the German police force? Where would England be if she had a national force and a militantly left-wing Home Secretary who didn't give a twopenny damn for anything but his Marxist ideals?

There was a knock on the door. 'Come in,' Radamski called out.

Superintendent Fingle entered. 'Sorry to interrupt you, sir, but the report's through of a security van gone missing after collecting over thirty thousand pounds from one of the banks in the High Street.'

'Is that all we know so far?'

'Yes, sir.'

'Surely, the vans are fitted with wireless?'

'Yes, sir, but I've been on to the firm's H.Q. and apparently there's been terrible static during a part of the morning. They received a message from this van to report it had collected the money and then nothing more. They've repeatedly tried to raise it without any success.'

'Have any of our cars met with undue static?'

'Only one, sir, and it wasn't quite enough to stop messages getting through. The car was a fair way away from the route the van took.'

'D'you know if the time of this static coincided with the time the van was on the road?'

'Yes, sir, it did. I've put out a general alarm and sent a car along the route.'

'Thanks for letting me know. Tell me if there are any developments, will you?'

The superintendent withdrew. Radamski stood up and walked across to the large-scale map on the wall which showed the borough limits.

· · · · ·

At three-thirty-five in the afternoon, Craig and Miller were called out to the old brick factory where the abandoned armoured van had been found. They drove there in the worn-out and rusting Humber that was allocated to them—the district police authority committee had not yet been able to provide the kind of equipment the regional crime squads needed.

Three police cars were parked in the lane and a uniformed constable stood guard by them. After Craig and Miller had identified themselves, he waved them on to park where they could.

They left the car and walked along to the factory. Detective Chief Inspector Barnard, looking very hot and even sourer than usual, called them over to where he stood. 'You'll work with the rest of them and not leave without reference to me.'

'Yes, sir,' said Miller.

'All right, carry on.'

They left and split up, Craig going to help with the close pattern search.

It was hot, dusty, boring, back-breaking work. The sun beat down on the men and even though they had all discarded their coats the sweat rolled down their faces and backs. The line moved slowly down the side of one oblong shaped kiln and up the side of the next. Every inch of ground had to be closely examined for anything that could have been left behind by the robbers and from time to time one of the men called the D.I. or the D.C.I. across to show him something on the ground. If there was the slightest possibility that this could be important, it was photographed, together with a ruler to give scale, and then taken over to the operations van, parked in the centre, to be listed and packed. Beyond the operations van, two detectives were painstakingly going over both the armoured van and the smaller van with the gas cylinders inside it for finger-prints.

Three-quarters of an hour later, Craig reached a small pile of bricks which were hidden behind long straw coloured grass which had grown up all around them. He parted the grass with a stick and studied each brick in turn. On the right-hand side of the pile was one that had been starred, recently to judge from the bright contrast in colour with the rest of the brick. He knelt down, after checking where his knees would go, and examined the brick more closely.

'Anything?' asked a man.

He turned, looked up, and recognised the detective inspector. 'I don't know yet, sir. It's just that this brick has been recently hit by something.'

The D.I. knelt by Craig and studied the brick. 'We're quite a way away from anything else we've found.'

'That mark's about the right height for a car to have made it, sir.'

'Yeah. Someone backing round who saw only a clump of grass and discovered the bricks by hitting 'em.' The D.I. stood up and turned to face the entrance to the factory. 'If they had their getaway car here or else came previously on a reconnaissance, they might very well have come in and backed round.'

He slowly walked forward and when he had gone four yards he came to a stop and stared intently at the ground. 'Smith,' he shouted.

A uniformed constable who had been standing by the side of the operations van started to come across. 'Shellac,' the D.I. called out.

The constable turned round and went into the operations van. He came out with a small aerosol tin which he brought over. The D.I. directed the tin at the ground and operated the spray, moving it across an area of four inches. He handed the tin back to the constable and knelt down to view the ground from several angles. Finally, he called over the detective sergeant, who was the photographer, and gave orders for the print to be photographed and the area to be fenced with white markers.

The D.I. returned to where Craig waited. 'A tyre mark,' he said. 'As indistinct as it could be, but there's a bit of a hollow with dust in it and the imprint's there. It'll give some sort of pattern, but I don't think they'll be able to lift it. All right, let's see if there's anything more here.'

They began a slow search of the bricks and the grass. Craig found a small flake of cream coloured paint, roughly star shaped, and less than a quarter of an inch in diameter.

The photographer, Detective Sergeant Harrolds, was called away from the tyre print. He came, muttering that even an overworked policeman could only do one job at a time.

The D.I. parted the grass. 'See that flake of paint?'

The detective sergeant nodded.

'Photograph it close to, then get back for shots of the whole site.'

'It's not exactly going to be easy.'

'You don't even find breathing easy.'

Harrolds smiled. He had the air of a licensed jester who had been in the force long enough to remember when all the bosses were mere coppers on the beat.

Craig helped Harrolds to take the photographs. Harrolds proved to be a perfectionist and it was over a quarter of an hour later before he was satisfied with his work. At the end of this time, Craig was ordered to go to the operations van for a container for the paint chip.

The operations van was hot and airless and the men inside were sweating, especially the wireless operator who was having trouble in getting a message through to H.Q. to ask the G.P.O. to come out and hook up a telephone.

A constable, his light blue shirt heavily stained under his arm-pits and down his chest, spoke to Craig. 'What's the order?'

'A container for a chip of paint. The smallest you've got.'

The constable opened a suitcase and brought out a plastic tube with a cork stopper. He tore free some plastic foam. 'Use a pen for making out the label if you can, chum.'

'Sure.' Craig took the tube and the foam. 'Is there any joy anywhere?'

'Not in my heart there isn't.' The constable mopped his forehead with a handkerchief. 'They've come up with two empty tins of gas, no finger-prints, a couple of lead-filled coshes, one covered in blood, no finger-prints, a noise baffler made out of a fibreglass bath, no finger-prints, two vans, no finger-prints, one constable's uniform, no finger-prints. I'll tell you, so far we don't . . .' He stopped as the detective chief inspector hurried into the operations van and demanded to know if anyone had done anything about laying on telephones.

Craig carried the plastic tube back to the small pile of bricks, lifted the paint chip into it, inserted the plastic foam to hold the chip against the wall of the tube and fixed the stopper. He handed the tube to the D.I. who wrote the date, time, and place on the label and added his signature. Craig took the tube back to the operations van. Whilst he was there, a constable brought in the three 'Diversion' and one 'Road Up' signs.

'No dabs,' said the newcomer. 'Not a flaming dab anywhere.'

'I reckon the job was pulled by armless apes,' said the constable who was manning the operations van.

'Have you heard how the blokes are?'

'One guard's about to collect his burial allowance from the

Health Service, one's got a stinking sore head, and the other three are conscious and coughing fit to bust a gut.'

'It's a rough, tough life.'

Craig left the van. He wondered how those two could treat the injuries so light-heartedly? Couldn't they visualise what the victims of such violence were suffering? He could, only too clearly, just as he had always been able to. This transference of identity was, he knew, both an asset and a liability to him as a detective. It enabled him cheerfully to undertake the most boring task because he could see how it would eventually help the victim of a crime, but it also meant that he became too emotionally involved.

As the hot sunshine covered him, Craig suddenly thought of Daphne. She loved the sun. She said that if he'd go and live somewhere on the Mediterranean, she'd come and join him and wouldn't bother too much about the blessing of clergy. As she put it, sunshine was a more valuable commodity than her virtue. Last year they had taken a short holiday together in Devon and it had rained every day.

He stood still and studied the scene around him. It was one which stemmed from violence. Men had robbed and beaten bloody other men. Eight weeks before he had been drafted to R.C.S., he had been on a rape case. The girl was young, attractive, and terribly shocked. At the time, he had imagined Daphne as the victim of the rape and the thought had made him sick. Yet how did you deal with such a revolting crime? Dusty would probably say castrate the rapist, but that was ridiculous. Perhaps even to imprison the man was really a waste of time.

Craig returned to the pile of bricks and continued the search, covering ground he knew had already been covered, but certain that no police officer had ever carried out too thorough a search.

· · · · ·

Miller walked the length of the hospital corridor, thick with characteristic smell of ether and illness. He feared hospitals.

Illness was something which reduced a man to helplessness and he had never been helpless in his life.

The porter had given him the number of McQueen's room and when he reached it, he knocked on the door. After a few seconds, it was opened by a woman in uniform. 'Excuse me, Nurse . . .' he began.

'Sister,' she corrected him stiffly.

'Sorry. I'm Detective Sergeant Miller. Can you tell me how McQueen is?'

'He's still unconscious. They'll be operating on him soon to try to find out the extent of the damage to the brain, but no one knows what the result'll be.' She stared at him. 'Why?' Her voice was high. 'Why were they so terribly brutal?'

He shrugged his shoulders.

'He could be paralysed for life. His wife was here a little earlier. She's a nice woman. She told me she's got two children and the youngest is only four and they're saving every penny to pay the house mortgage. She's terrified that if he's too badly injured the firm won't keep him on and they'll get behind on the mortgage repayments.'

He said nothing. It was a story he had heard so often before. Detectives spent a lot of their working lives next to tragedy. If all the abolitionists and half-baked intellectuals, who thought the robber was so much more clever and important than the robbed, could be made to see what crime meant in terms of blood, bone, gut and misery, then perhaps they'd shut their bloody mouths and start thinking for a change.

'What?' said the sister.

'How d'you mean?'

'I thought you said something?'

He shook his head. 'I was just thinking how I'd like to string the bastards up.' He didn't apologise for the use of the word. 'You said he might be paralysed—what are the odds?'

'Pretty bad. D'you know who did it?'

'Not yet. Someone will be along tomorrow to see if he's conscious and can help.'

'There's absolutely no point to anyone coming before Monday at the earliest.'

'O.K. I'll tell them that.'

He thanked her, turned, and walked back along the corridor. As he was going down the stairs to the main entrance, he passed a woman of about thirty whose face expressed a deep and heartbreaking grief. Her face haunted his mind and kept him wondering whether she was McQueen's wife.

. . . . .

Haggard climbed out of bed. He stared down at Florence, who was naked. Right now, she irritated him because of the way she was acting. A brass was normally hard by nature—she had to be, or go under—but when a brass attached herself to a man she became so soft she was like putty, provided the man had the sense to remain hard. It was a love/hate, kick/be kicked, spit/be spat on relationship. A brass angered him when she went soft, even though if she hadn't he'd have knocked her to hell and back to break her.

'Take me up to The Smoke,' she pleaded.

'I told you.'

'Why? Why won't you?'

He turned and began to dress. At first, he'd refused to take her just to annoy her, but then she kept on and on until he became angry. She'd used her body to try to make him change his mind, but although he'd accepted her bribe he wasn't fool enough to be bribed by it. As he pulled on his shirt, he thought that when he was in London he'd find himself a brass, a real slick expensive one.

'You're going to see another woman,' she said shrilly, as if she had read his mind.

'That's right.'

She cursed him. He smiled. One of the real genuine pleasures in life was to plan one woman whilst another was around, screaming for attention.

'Why d'you want another woman?'

'Variety.'

'Don't I know enough?'

'You're reasonable—for a beginner.' He laughed. Now she

50

was really spitting. She reckoned she could give lessons to anyone, even Messalina, who she certainly had never heard of. He opened the door of the built-in cupboard and studied his nine suits and four sets of sports clothes. What to wear in London? He noticed the suit he'd been wearing that morning and he was once again warmed by the thought of the successful robbery. His gaze moved on to the grey suit which had cost eighty quid in London. That was his smartest and he'd wear it.

6

SATURDAY'S weather was the antithesis of Friday's. The sun had vanished, the sky was overcast with dark bellied clouds, and most of the time there was a light drizzle.

In a dingy public house in Power Street, at the back of Piccadilly Circus, a detective sergeant ordered two whiskies. The publican poured out two doubles and said they were on the house. The detective thanked him and carried the glasses across to the table at which Yarnley sat.

Yarnley had once been a cat burglar. There were some who said that in his heyday he could have climbed straight up Nelson's Column, no hands either. Perhaps he was showing off and not using his hands when he fell fifteen feet from the side of a house in Hampstead. The concrete path broke so many bones in his body that his case was mentioned in two medical textbooks. He became a permanent cripple and crippled cat burglars find life hard. In order to exist he took to informing.

The detective passed Yarnley a glass.

'I've got news,' said Yarnley.

'If it's as up to date as last time, don't bother.'

' 'Onest to Gawd, this is real.'

The detective continued to look carelessly indifferent.

'The news is worth a tenner.'

'Not unless it concerns the Crown Jewels.'

Yarnley leaned forward and dropped his voice. 'A bloke of interest is flush.'

The detective finished his drink and twisted the glass round by its stem. 'Drink up.'

Yarnley drained his glass with noisy swallows. The detective took the glasses over to the counter, careful to remember which was whose, and accepted two more whiskies from the publican. When he returned to the table, he brought out a packet of cigarettes which he laid on the table.

' 'E was real flush,' said Yarnley. 'Throwing it around.'

The detective lit a cigarette and blew out the match. If the information was genuine, he'd be able to claim from the central fund whatever he now paid out to Yarnley: if it wasn't, he wouldn't get a penny back. 'Lots of people are flush these days. It's the Welfare State.'

'But I saw 'is roll. It was thicker'n my fist.'

'Who was it?'

'A bloke I was on the Moor with. He got chokey for belting a screw.'

'So he's a ripe villain. What's his name?'

Yarnley fidgeted with his glass, drank, put the glass back on the table and took a cigarette from the opened packet. 'It's worth a tenner.' He searched his pockets for a light.

'What's his name?' repeated the detective, as he slid a box of matches across the table.

'I . . . I know 'im but I don't remember 'is name.'

'Come on.'

'No. That's genuine.'

The detective cursed.

'Look, Mister, 'e was with Gertie: blonde Gertie. She'll know 'im.'

'Where's her turf these days?'

'Down 'Apworth Street, above the paper shop.'

The detective gave Yarnley a pound and curtly refused to add anything to that amount unless blonde Gertie could remember the man's name. The detective left the pub, walked along to the end of Power Street and turned into Hapworth Street. The newsagent's was the ninth shop along the road and on the right of it was a door giving access to a flight of stairs. The detective climbed the stairs and knocked on the door at the head of them. He was let into the waiting-room by an Irish maid who asked him if he had an appointment. He said he had. Whilst he waited, he picked up one of the copies of *Vogue* on the table and stared with near incredulity at the photographs of models wearing the latest fashions.

The Irish maid came back and showed him into the luxuriously appointed bedroom, with mirrors on every wall and on the ceiling. 'Hullo, Gertie, how's life?'

Gertie swore, fluently and violently. She was a strikingly attractive blonde, who earned enough to be able to view the Prime Minister's salary with scorn.

The detective listened patiently until she stopped, whereupon he asked her who her rich customer had been the previous night. She said he was a South American tin millionaire and the detective said she was a liar. There was a silence. Gertie said he was bad for business. He replied he was sorry, but duty was duty. After another and longer silence, she said Haggard had taken her to dinner at the most expensive restaurant in town and later had paid up without argument, which was more than could be said for some who called themselves gentlemen, but that he was far too vicious. She offered to show the bruises, but the detective said that business came before pleasure.

* * * * *

Detective Sergeant Miller looked up as the police cadet came into the R.C.S. office.

'There's a message for your outfit, Sarge. Just come in on the Telex.'

'Thanks.' Miller took the sheet of paper and read the message as the cadet left. 'All sections, R.C.S., origin A.C.C. Thomas Haggard, convictions armed robbery, etc., ref. 344/TH, spending heavily London. Present whereabouts believed Home Counties. Age 33, scar right cheek, tip left little finger missing. Full description, Blue H143. Advise whereabouts.'

Miller stood up and crossed to one of the filing cabinets—only filled that morning. He brought out a blue folder, marked H100—150. Inside were potted histories and notes on *modus operandi* of all criminals convicted of violent crimes during the past five years throughout the country. There was a full description of Haggard with a badly reproduced photograph.

Miller carried the folder back to his desk. Whoever pulled the job the previous day would be flush all right. Haggard's record said that he was clever, brutally careless about the means he used to achieve his object, and a recidivist. He'd been out of prison for just long enough to plan a job like yesterday's.

Miller telephoned the D.C.I. and reported the R.C.S. message. Barnard formally thanked him. Miller said either he or Craig would have a word with forces in the sub-region and Barnard again formally thanked him.

Since this was the first time a group message had been received, Miller decided to send Craig round to the various police forces or divisional commands, rather than use the telephone. The sooner the advantages of co-operation were realised, the sooner co-operation would be received: the personal touch would be more likely to be successful in gaining this.

Craig used the old Humber to drive to the various divisional headquarters that lay within the sub-region of R.C.S. control and he was received in ways that varied from indifference to friendliness. At Telton, the reception was not only friendly, but also informative.

The detective sergeant was a tall, thin man who, when thinking deeply, had a habit of flicking his lips with his fingers. 'Haggard? Something tells me . . . Jackie'll know. He knows everything.' He picked up the internal telephone and dialled a number. He spoke briefly, listened a while, thanked the other man and replaced the receiver. 'Our station sergeant recognised Haggard the other day and made a few discreet enquiries to find out what he's doing in Telton. He's living in one of the new luxury flats. There's a woman with him who usually works the town, but while she's with him she's off the streets.' He leaned back in his chair. 'Is he a possible for the armoured van job yesterday?'

'London says that last night he was spending money like water.'

'Has anyone picked up a lead that might incriminate him?

'The last time I heard, there weren't any leads.'

'The professionals are getting more professional every day. What's your next move?'

Craig asked if it was possible to find out what colour Haggard's car was and the other replied that it should be easy since there weren't any garages to the flats and the cars had to be parked in the forecourt.

After being given directions, Craig left the police station and walked along to the main road which was almost solid with week-end traffic, despite the continuing drizzle. He cut through the small memorial gardens and came to the tall, match-box style, block of flats.

There were a dozen cars parked in the forecourt, ranging from a Mini to a couple of Jaguars. Only one was cream coloured and that was an American car of very large proportions.

Craig studied the Buick Riviera, number 545 PKM. The colour was, as near as he could remember it, the same as the tiny chip of paint he had found in the brick factory.

He went slowly round the car, looking for damaged paintwork. Just above the rear bumper, he found a small star shaped area where a chip had been taken out.

He left the forecourt and walked back to the main street and a telephone kiosk. He telephoned Frindhurst police station and spoke to Miller.

'Haggard lives here, in a block of luxury flats. The cars have to be parked outside and one of 'em is a cream coloured Buick, registration number five four five PKM. There's no knowing at the moment it is Haggard's, but I'm certain the colour matches the chip found at the brick factory. On the rear of the boot a chip of paint has been knocked off and the shape's right.'

'O.K. I'll check the number with the registration people, if any of 'em are working on a Saturday. Right now, go and knock another chip off for comparison tests.'

'What?'

'Knock another chip off and don't worry about it being too big.'

'Hell, Dusty, I can't do that even before we're certain it's his car.'

'You knock a chip off that bloody car and stop worrying about what you can't do.' Miller cut the connection.

Craig left the telephone kiosk. The drizzle had increased in intensity and he raised the collar of his mackintosh. He cursed Miller. Policemen were divided into those who kept within the rules and those who didn't. Sometimes, a man changed sides because each man had his own morality scale. He had always been quite certain that justice had to be administered legally, or it ceased to have the virtue of justice. If the police found it more and more difficult successfully to serve justice—the new judges' rules were an example of the increased difficulties—then it was not for the police to try to circumvent such difficulties: they must accept the fact that their hands were being legally tied. Only a change of law must be allowed to untie them.

It could so easily turn out that Haggard had not done the Frindhurst job. Then, an illegal trespass to his goods would be doubly wrong. The fact that Haggard had never himself operated within the law was, in this context, irrelevant.

He hesitated. If he returned to Frindhurst and said he'd stuck by the letter of the law, Dusty would swear, pick up the telephone, and ask someone in Telton to belt the Buick a sharp blow and so secure a sample of the paintwork. There was bound to be more than one policeman in Telton who would think, with Miller, that there was nothing wrong in such action. His own refusal to do as he had been ordered would result in a short delay, nothing more. He smiled briefly. Since when had virtue ever stood a ghost of a chance against vice?

He returned to the Buick and used his penknife to force off a chip of paint, which he put in the envelope of the last letter Daphne had written him. When he pocketed the envelope and turned, he saw an old tramp, standing on the pavement, watching.

Craig walked out of the forecourt. The tramp stood still, but his head moved round as he watched and water dripped unheeded from his torn and dirty cap on to his stubbled cheek.

Haggard and Florence took the lift down to the ground floor of the block of flats. He hurried out and she had to run to keep up with him. Haggard was angry and determined to show it. The stupid cow had groaned and moaned so hard that in the end, for the sake of peace, he had finally agreed to take her to Brighton. Ever since he'd got back from London, she'd been playing the same record: what had he done, what brass had he gone with, what was wrong with her, Florence? His answers had done nothing to ease her jealous fury.

He reached the Buick and unlocked the driver's door, on the near-side because there were no right-hand drive Rivieras. He had a pile-driving headache and his mouth and throat were open incinerators. Blonde Gertie had been worth every penny of the seventy quid, but she'd left him feeling as if he'd taken a header into a close-coupled wringer. He must be getting old. Five years ago, a week with Gertie wouldn't have twisted a hair on his head. Age was the one thing he couldn't fight. 'Are you coming, or aren't you?' he shouted at Florence.

She hammered on the other door to show she couldn't open it and he leaned across and unlocked it.

'I can't open a locked door,' she complained, as she climbed in.

'Tell me something you can do.'

'I can do anything she can.'

Haggard switched on the engine. He put the lever to drive, released the handbrake, and accelerated. The car, easily handled because of the power steering, swept round in a tight semi-circle. For the first time that day, he felt good. A driving-wheel had all the thrills of a woman's curves and a powerful engine had all the responses. One of these days he'd go to Brands Hatch and take a belt round the track in a racing car. He was a born driver, like Stirling Moss. Only Nouvolari had ever been in the same class as Moss.

A dirty old tramp stepped in front of the car, as if trying to commit suicide. Haggard slammed on the brakes and the car screeched to a halt. Florence cracked her head on the windscreen. He pressed the button which lowered his window and began to shout at the tramp.

'Only doin' you a favour,' whined the tramp.

'You do me a favour, then, and jump into a coffin.'

'It was your car. 'E scraped some paint off, that's what. I saw 'im.'

For the first time, Haggard realised that this was not some bleary meths drinker trying to bum. He pulled on the handbrake and switched off the windscreen wipers.

'I ain't 'ad a bite for a week, Mister,' said the tramp.

'You've got a long way to go before you die from starvation.'

' 'Ow about somethin' to warm me blood?'

'Who was mucking around with this car?'

The tramp, trying to escape the determined drizzle, buried himself more deeply within the tattered coat he was wearing and a corner of newpaper—used as padding—incongruously rose up the back of his neck.

Haggard pulled a roll of money from his pocket and peeled off a five-pound note. He held it up.

The tramp came up to the car. 'I was standing there,' he said, and pointed along the pavement.

'Get on about the car.'

'This bloke, younger than you, like, comes to your car, 'as a look at the number and writes it down in a little book, 'e does.'

'How d'you know that's what he was doing?'

'Weren't no doubt.' The tramp had become slightly cocky in manner. ' 'E starts looking around the paintwork, reaches the back, bends down and 'as a butchers at something real close to. After that, 'e leaves. I ain't nothing to do, so I waits. 'E comes back, takes a knife from 'is pocket and scrapes a bit of paint off and puts it in an envelope.'

Haggard sat still, both hands on the steering-wheel. The five-pound note was scrumpled up between his hand and the wheel.

' 'Ow about me money?' said the tramp.

Haggard threw the note out of the window. The wind caught it and carried it away over the bonnet of the car. The tramp, showing amazing agility for one so apparently decrepit, ran after it.

'It was the Law,' said Florence.

'It wasn't.' Why should the Law bother about his car? Yet who else would note down the number or scrape off a bit of paint?

'It was the Law,' she repeated.

He told her to belt up. The Law couldn't know he'd done the job yesterday. They might suspect: they might say that only a right clever bastard did the job so Thomas Haggard, Esquire, was a natural, but suspicions meant nothing. Where would the paint from his car fit into the suspicions?

'She grassed on you,' shouted Florence, 'that's what.'

'Who?' Then he realised she was on again about blonde Gertie. All that women could think about was other women. Hadn't she the sense to realise that Gertie wasn't of any importance compared with a scraping of paint?

Why scrape paint off his car?

7

THAT evening, Craig was invited to supper with the Miller family. He was surprised to discover the kind of person Violet Miller was. From the way her husband had spoken about her, Craig had expected her to be domineering, self-confident to the point of brashness, and interfering. He had imagined her to be heavily built with a face of granite-like toughness. Instead, she was a small woman, younger than her husband, attractive and elegant even if all her clothes were mass-produced. She had a natural reserve which was almost shyness, but with Craig this reserve soon disappeared. He had the wit to realise that husband and wife were still very much in love and that Miller's attitude was no more than an attempt to conceal his emotions.

The meal was a noisy one mainly because of the two teen-age children, both overflowing with vitality, who were going out to a party given by a friend of the daughter's who had moved with her family to Frindhurst two years before.

After the meal was over and the children had left, the other three settled in the sitting-room.

'Albert told me you may be going to the college in Hampshire and on to a university,' said Violet Miller, as she sat down.

'I hope so,' answered Craig. 'But it all depends how I get on now and what happens in the sergeants' exams.'

'I expect you'd like to go on from there to the university and get a degree?'

'I most certainly would. Goodness only knows whether I'm bright enough, though.'

'Bright enough for what?' muttered Miller. 'Catching villains?'

She smiled. 'Albert's never forgiven that man—wasn't it Lord Trenchard?—who tried to get public school boys into the force before the war. D'you remember, Bert, how you swore you'd buy an old Etonian tie and use it to keep up your trousers if ever you served under one of them. My husband's a genuine socialist, John, he doesn't want anyone else to have what he hasn't.'

'That's nonsense,' protested Miller.

'Your politics or your reactions?' She smiled as she rested her hand on his. 'When you get an idea into your head nothing'll shift it, not even complete proof to the contrary. If you saw one of Lord Trenchard's white hopes rescuing an unconscious man from a lion's den, you'd swear the lion was only a circus act.'

'I'll tell you something . . .'

'You won't, not while John's here. You might shock him.'

'Just answer me one question. Is the crime rate going up, or isn't it?'

'It is, because the policemen of the old school failed to do their job properly.'

'Woman, your arguments are . . .'

'You're not to call me woman.'

'Why not?'

'I know perfectly well what policemen mean when they talk about women. I may be a lot of things, but I'm still reasonably virtuous.'

Miller chuckled. 'More's the pity. They say there's nothing like experience.'

'I am going to change the conversation.' She turned. 'John, would you like some coffee?'

'I'd love some, please.'

'Bert?'

'Yes, I'll have some, love.'

'Good, then you can go and make it.'

Grumbling loudly, Miller got up from the settee and left the room. She spoke almost shyly to Craig. 'I do hope you go to the college and do well so you can go on to the university. I'm sure it's a wonderful idea. Or do you really think I don't know what I'm talking about? I never know how much wives are meant to understand about their husbands' work. Up at H.Q. we had to live in one of those houses on the police estate and most of the other wives seemed to go out of their way not to know anything. Some of them actually seemed ashamed that their husbands were policemen. I've always been proud of it. I'm sure you're proud of being in the force?'

'Yes, I am.'

Miller returned to the room in time to hear Craig's answer. 'Yes you are what? What's my beloved wife twisted you into admitting?'

'Proud of being in the force.'

Miller, out of tune, began to sing Rule Britannia. His wife interrupted the noise to say that she could hear the kettle boiling and would he go out and turn it off. When he reached the kettle, he discovered it was nowhere near boiling.

Craig left the house at ten-thirty and Violet Miller, with obvious sincerity, pressed him to come again soon. He answered, with equal sincerity, that nothing would give him greater pleasure.

As he walked back to his own digs, through streets that were damp from the rain which had only just ceased, he thought about the sense of peace and happiness the Millers were able to project even after the disturbance of so recent a move to an entirely new district and to a house where they were merely lodgers. He was certain that Daphne and he would live within the same sense of peace and happiness. Already, there existed between them the quietness of deep affection in which neither of them had to strive to make himself or herself attractive to the other. He suddenly thought that Daphne had been one hundred and one per cent right. They should have married before he was posted to R.C.S. and then he wouldn't be returning to miserable digs with only the gaunt crow of a landlady to greet him.

· · · · ·

Radamski was in his office on Sunday morning. He was no half-time chief constable, treating the job as an annoying penalty to be paid the minimum amount of lip service: he conscientiously worked to the best of his considerable ability. The robbery was a brutal one which, if humanly possible, had to be solved. Because the Frindhurst police force wasn't big enough to deal with that crime and all the others recently committed, he had to decide, among other things, which relatively minor crimes were to go uninvestigated. No police force in the country was big enough to deal adequately with all crimes.

The detective chief inspector made his report at ten o'clock. Radamski knew Barnard to be efficient, but found him decidedly a cold fish. The chief constable liked a man who could relax at the right moment and maybe crack a joke or two. The only jokes Barnard ever made were quite unintentional.

''Morning, Barnard. Sit you down and have a cigarette?'

'No thanks, sir, I've a lot to get on with. The report on the two chips of car paint has come through from London. Spectroscopic analysis shows they are identical, so the chip found in the brickyard came from Haggard's car.'

Radamski lit a cigarette. 'Then we can be certain who it was,' he said quietly. 'Not that we've anything much in the way of proof yet. Haggard's car has been in the brickyard, but at the very best that's only confirmatory evidence, acting on the laws of probability, unless we can prove it was actually around during the robbery. And that, surely, is most unlikely?'

'I agree, sir.'

'What's your next move?'

'Put an urgent call through to the Telton police, sir, asking for any help they can give and get the two men from R.C.S. to work with them.'

'Good.' Radamski spoke evenly, but his voice was hard. 'We've got to get them, you know.'

'We will, sir.'

Craig was at Telton central police station, talking to the detective sergeant, when a message came through that a British Rail car-park attendant had just reported that a Jaguar saloon car had been left in the car-park over the week-end, that it was unlocked, and that it seemed to have been abandoned even though in excellent order.

The detective sergeant suggested Craig should go with him to look at the car. The men who did the Frindhurst robbery would have used stolen cars and Jaguars were a favourite with all grades of criminals. The two detectives drove to the car-park, examined the car, took the number, and checked by telephone with the police station whether that number was on the county list of stolen cars. It wasn't. Craig said he would see whether the number was on the national list, held by R.C.S. A quick telephone call brought the information that it was. The Jaguar had been stolen from Brighton on Thursday evening.

The detective sergeant immediately gave orders for a clip-on steering-wheel—to protect any finger-prints on the car's steering-wheel—to be brought from the station, together with a selection of ignition keys.

Craig began the search of the ground around the Jaguar. He checked on the grass which grew up around the chestnut paling fence and then got down on hands and knees to look under the cars on either side. Under the third car to the right he saw a glove. By reaching out at full stretch, he was able to pick this up with the tips of two fingers. It was a cotton glove, of the kind commonly sold for gardening. The back was filthy where a car's tyre had run over it, but the palm was relatively clean. In one corner was a dull, brown patch which was almost certainly blood. Craig called across the detective sergeant, who brought with him a large plastic bag.

* * * * *

Now that they knew the mechanics of the robbery, the police began to make progress. There were no finger-prints on the Jaguar, but they did find a small item of wireless equipment which had fallen down the back of the passenger seat. It was sent away for identification. Haggard was now being watched and just after dusk the detective constable saw him come out of the flats and climb into his cream coloured Buick. The detective hurried to his own black Austin and drove off, trying to trail the Buick. Normally, he would probably have failed in his task, but two factors now helped him: the Buick was readily identifiable even at a distance, and the journey was a short one. The Buick came to a stop in one of the meaner streets of Telton, before a house that had not been painted in years. The detective happened to know that Soapy Brown lived in that house. Soapy was supposed to be going straight now, but that was as maybe: more importantly, there wasn't a torch artist for miles to compare with him. The detective parked his car and waited. A Mini drew up behind the Buick and two men climbed out of it. The detective didn't know the smaller of the two, but the larger man was Ringo Grant. This was truly a gathering of the clans.

* * * * *

Tuesday morning was sunny, with a sky dotted with woolly puffs of cumulus that sent shadows racing across the ground. Two of the daily newspapers contained articles dealing with the Frindhurst robbery. Both articles were critical of the police and the longer one listed all the major unsolved crimes in the country over the past month. The police, said the writer, were failing to move with the times and adapt their techniques to the increased sophistication of the criminals. The writer omitted to mention the astonishing cost of new techniques.

In London, after working for fourteen hours, one of the civilian forensic scientists completed his task. Wearily, he sat down and wrote out his report. The stain on the glove had been dried blood and he had managed to type this blood down to show it had an LU (a+b+) factor, a factor possessed by only one person in every half-million. Although he did not then know it, he had proved—unless there had been a fantastic coincidence—that the blood on the glove came from the injured guard, since McQueen's blood had been shown to have the same LU (a+b+) factor.

At twelve-fourteen that morning, Detective Inspector Glaze of the Telton police and Detective Sergeant Miller drove to the block of luxury flats. They went in and took the lift up to the fifth floor. Glaze, a large man with a roly-poly face, knocked on the door of flat 5A.

Florence opened the door of the flat. There was no need for either of the callers to announce his profession. 'What d'you want?' she asked shrilly.

'Is Haggard in?' Glaze asked.

'No.'

The force of her denial was ruined when Haggard stepped into the hall to see who the callers were.

'You're living in style,' said Glaze, as he entered.

'Who told you to come in?' demanded Haggard.

'Your loving wife.'

Florence began to call the detective several obscene things.

'Belt up,' said Haggard.

There was a short silence.

'Busy these days?' asked Glaze.

'Sure.' Haggard's face was expressionless.

'Busy doing what?'

'This and that.'

'Must be paying to be able to afford to live in a place like this.'

'I manage.'

'I couldn't begin to afford to live here.'

'What's the matter? Not being offered enough bung?' Immediately, Haggard regretted this characteristic outburst of malevolence.

'Are you offering us a bribe?'

'Why should I?'

'You might be soft enough to think that's one way of wriggling out of your last job.'

'What last job?'

'You don't need me to spell things out.'

'I don't need you.'

'Thirty-three thousand one hundred and fifty-two pounds is a lot of money, even in this day and age of train robberies.'

'Is it?' In his trouser pocket, Haggard clenched his right hand. Until now, with a little wishful thinking and despite the man who'd taken paint from the Buick, it had been possible to believe the Law knew nothing about him and the Frindhurst job. That was no longer so. How'd they found out? Someone had grassed. That must be the answer. The job had been done too cleverly for them to find out any other way: too bloody cleverly for any dumb split to discover. When he found out who'd done the grassing, he'd stripe the bloke so hard his own mother would walk past him, thinking him a piece of old beef.

'Have you friends in this town?' asked Glaze.

'I've friends everywhere, being so popular.'

'Soapy Brown, maybe?'

'I know him.' Had Soapy grassed? That little runt'd grass on his own wife if it were made worth while.

'You've done time together, haven't you?'

'I can't remember.'

'What about Ringo Grant?'

'What about him?'

'Do you know him?'

'Suppose you tell me?'

'I will tell you something, then.'

'Don't bother. I'm not curious.'

'I'll have a little bet that when we ask you for an alibi, you'll name one of them.'

Haggard silently cursed them. Like all splits, when they thought they were on top, they jeered.

'As a matter of interest, where were you?' asked Glaze.

'When?'

'When the armoured car job was being done, of course.'

'What's it worry you where I was?'

'Are you serious?'

Haggard swore.

'Where were you between eleven and one last Friday?'

'Are you charging me with the job?'

'Not yet.'

'Then come asking again when you are.'

'You'll be on the line for preventive detention this time, won't you?'

Haggard, using every ounce of self-control, forced himself to keep his explosive temper in check.

'You near killed a man,' went on Glaze. 'I wouldn't mind betting you get close to ten years.'

'Someone been hurt?'

'You belted McQueen so hard he's still lying unconscious in bed in hospital.'

'It's a tough life.'

'You're on the way to finding just how tough it can get.'

'Why come and worry me with his problems? He asked for it. He wasn't forced to dress up in a nice blue uniform and play at being a brave guard.'

'He was doing his job,' said Glaze, speaking tightly.

'Then he can't rightly complain if he suffers a bit in the line of duty, like.'

'Suffers a bit? He may never recover consciousness. He may go on lying in bed like a living corpse. D'you call that suffering just a little bit? Have you thought about his wife and kids? What's going to happen to them?'

'Married, is he? Now that's nice for him. Comforting to have a wife and family, isn't it?' Haggard smiled, showing his white, even teeth. He'd made the splits lose their tempers. You could always get a split steamed up over a thing like McQueen: they got all sorry for their brothers, just like the Holy Joes in prison who almost dropped down dead from excitement at all their sorrow for their brothers.

'His wife's frantic,' said Miller, his voice harsh from impotent anger.

'Women do get het-up.'

'Where were you last Friday morning?' said Glaze harshly.

'Last Friday? Last Friday?'

'Come on, where were you?'

'I know. I was in bed with Flo here. She's good in bed.'

Glaze hesitated, then turned and crossed to the door. Miller followed him.

'Going so soon?' asked Haggard mockingly. 'Goodbye, my darlings.'

'Au revoir. If you know what that means.'

Haggard stared at the door after it had been closed behind them. Who'd grassed? Soapy Brown? He'd stripe Soapy, he'd kill the little runt. Denton? Denton had a yellow streak a mile wide. Denton could have fouled up the job when he went soft and wouldn't hit the guard. Denton called himself educated, which meant he'd always let the next bloke down. Grant? Grant would never grass. Someone had grassed: the job was too bloody cleverly done for the splits to have found out any other way.

. . . . .

Leston, the driver of the armoured van, had been discharged from hospital on the Saturday morning. There were eight stitches in his scalp and he had a king-sized headache. He hardly slept Saturday night and through Sunday morning the pain throbbed through his head in never-ending waves. When Craig and a uniformed constable entered his house, near Blecester, he met them with bitter complaints at the police for not having prevented the robbery. His wife, driven almost to despair by worry and his temper, left the room to make tea.

Craig took several photographs from a large envelope and handed them to Leston. 'We'd like you to look through these, if you will, and see if you recognise anyone?'

'Am I likely to?'

'I couldn't say.'

'What I mean is, is there a photo here of the bloke what did the robbery and was dressed as a copper?'

'I can't answer that question.'

The constable, who had been in the force a long time, silently wondered just how difficult Craig wanted to make his job for himself.

Leston began to look through the photographs. Almost immediately, he dropped one and automatically reached down to pick it up. A fierce pain stabbed through his head. He groaned, leaned back in his chair, and closed his eyes. Craig picked up the photograph and put it on Leston's lap, with the others.

After a while, Leston recovered to the point where he opened his eyes once more. He looked through the photographs, each of which showed a man both full and side face. 'None of these blokes was him: like I said, he had a moustache.'

'Try imagining all those blokes with moustaches,' replied Craig patiently.

Leston looked ridiculously puzzled, as if this was the first time the possibility of a false moustache had occurred to him. He went through the photographs again, stopped at one towards the end, held it at arm's length, half closed his eyes, and studied it for some time. 'It could be this bloke.'

Craig took the photograph. It was of Haggard.

'Have I picked out the right bloke?' asked Leston eagerly.

'You're the only one who can say that.'

'Well, is it the bloke what you think did the job?'

Craig did not answer, but took more photographs from a second envelope and handed them across. 'Try these now.'

Again, Leston picked out the photograph of Haggard—taken three years before the first one—but again the identification was not at all strong. As Craig grimly thought, in a court of law this identification would not begin to stand up to sharp cross-examination.

Mrs. Leston returned to the room with tea on a tray. She asked her husband how he felt and wearily listened to a long and self-pitying answer.

The two detectives left the house a quarter of an hour later and Craig drove back to Frindhurst, after dropping the constable at Blecester police station. Miller was back in the R.C.S. room.

'Any luck?' asked Miller.

Craig sat down on his desk and shrugged his shoulders. 'Leston identified Haggard's photo, but only with a lot of "I thinks" and "Buts". No one's going to make much of that identification in court.'

Miller tilted his chair back until he could rest his heels on the desk. 'We know Haggard did it, but how in the hell are we going to prove that with the evidence so weak? I'd like to take the judges and stuff the laws of evidence down their throats.'

'Why?'

'Why? Because the laws are always on the side of the villain. And you try and argue round that one. How many villains have you seen even in your short time get off and walk around as bold as brass because the laws of evidence stuck up for them and not for the truth?'

'You know the saying: better that ten guilty men should go free than one innocent man be convicted.'

'That makes me want to puke. Suppose we don't find any better evidence? Where are we? I'll tell you. One guard smashed into a senseless hulk, thirty-three thousand quid missing, and Haggard walking around and living like a lord. You ought to have a look at his flat. Luxury! And that's where villaining gets you these days because the laws of evidence are so soft.'

'You can't have judgement by suspicion,' replied Craig, almost wearily. 'Did you get anything useful out of Haggard?'

Miller took a packet of cigarettes from his pocket and threw a cigarette across to Craig. 'The two of us were bashing our heads against brick walls. Haggard just stood back and jeered at us for getting worked up over McQueen. I just can't understand the mentality, John. I just bloody can't. Men like Haggard are professional criminals by choice and nothing on God's earth'll ever change 'em. They look on prison as an occupational hazard and if the ratio is three inside to one outside, spending money like water, it's O.K. with them: that I can understand. But their disregard for other people, their utter callous disregard for anyone else, that's what I just can't begin to understand. It didn't matter to Haggard that McQueen may be a permanent cabbage, that his family's going to live through hell . . . that just didn't touch him. If I was a crook, I'd steal without worrying overmuch because most things are insured. But I couldn't smash a man into a bloody pulp. I'd be thinking of someone smashing me and how the Missus would live then and who'd find the money to bring up the kids. Haggard's not human, not like you and me. The topping shed's all that'll ever stop him.'

Craig knew that nothing he could answer would make sense to the other.

'We've got to get the bastard,' muttered Miller.

8

THE counter assistant in a wireless and electrical equipment store in Holborn, catering especially for the home builder, took the small piece of equipment from the detective and studied it briefly. He looked up and over the tops of his tortoiseshell framed glasses. 'Yes, we sold that.'

'How can you be so certain?'

'D'you see this mark?' The assistant used the point of a pencil to indicate a small cross in red paint. 'We put that on everything we sell as a check.'

'Good enough. What precisely is this thing?'

'A cut-and-shut transistor. You won't see many because they're not used much. If two, four, or six—always an even number—are wired up in series in a transmitter they send out a positive gale of noise like static. They're at the heart of a lot of anti-bugging devices. If you've got a set with these in it, there isn't a microphone can begin to break through the row.'

The detective constable from R.C.S., central region, wrote quickly in his notebook. 'If you don't sell many, there's just a chance you can remember selling this one, if it was recent?'

'There's more than a chance. I can tell you, I sold it last Thursday—I know, because that's the day Mr. Tibor was in to look at the books. A man came in and asked for four. They were the only ones we had in the place. I remember wondering what he wanted them for, but didn't say anything, of course. Tape recorders turn up in the most peculiar places these days and some blokes need to be on their guard.' The assistant tittered. 'Husbands can get very jealous, they tell me.'

'Would you recognise the buyer?'

'I'm sure I would. I've a good memory for faces.'

'You're being very helpful. Someone will be along with some photos for you to look through.' The detective replaced the notebook in his pocket. 'Just one thing. How can you be so certain this transistor isn't one you sold a long time ago?'

'Well I . . . I suppose I was rather jumping to conclusions, but I don't think we've sold any others for months. Like I said, they're a very occasional line.'

'Thanks very much, then.' The detective constable left the shop and walked along to Holborn Tube station.

At nine-seventeen Wednesday morning, the assistant looked through a number of photographs and, without any hesitation whatsoever, picked out one of Ringo Grant.

.   .   .   .   .

At ten-forty-two, Wednesday morning, Miller and Craig went to Frindhurst hospital. Outside McQueen's room, they met a sister. Miller asked if there was any change in McQueen's condition.

She shook her head. 'The operation was as successful as it could be, but they discovered the brain damage was too extensive to allow any sort of repair. He's just lying there, unconscious.'

'Why the hell didn't they let the knife slip?' muttered Miller.

The sister appeared not to have heard him.

Craig wondered about the wife. Had her mind yet broken through the rough comfort of the numbness of the first terrible shock? What was it like to know a day when one's husband left the house as fit as a fiddle and then next to see him in a hospital bed, a human cabbage, unable to move, talk, see, or hear?

Miller spoke again. 'Do the doctors think he'll ever recover consciousness?'

She sighed. 'Eventually he might, if you can call it consciousness.'

'Can we go in to see him?' asked Miller.

'Why? He's just lying there.'
'I want to see him.'
'But . . .?'
'If you don't mind.'

She said nothing more and Miller led the way into the room. McQueen lay on his back, his head in the centre of the pillow, the sheet and single blanket tucked exactly and neatly over him. His head was bandaged down to his eyes. There was nothing to show whether he was still living.

'D'you know why we're here?' demanded Miller.

'No,' answered Craig.

'So that you can have a look at the other side of the coin. Things get a bit different when you stop talking about them and are brought face to face with them.'

'I don't understand,' said Craig, which was a lie.

'Then just have a bloody good look at this poor swine and remember he's got a family. D'you know why he's there? Can you look beyond all your high and wide ideals and understand he's lying there because the law's soft and doesn't care about protecting the innocent? Why d'you think Haggard was so carelessly brutal? It was because he didn't care whether McQueen lived or died as it wouldn't make a twopenny damn of difference. The punishment wouldn't be any different.'

'But . . .'

'Your kind of arguments stink when there's a bloke like this lying around in a hospital.'

'You don't . . .'

'There's another little thing you might think about. It just so happens we know who did it and . . .'

'You think you know.'

'We know. Don't be such a bloody fool. We know. Yet what happens? Nothing. We know, yet we haven't the kind of evidence the court demands. The law says that Haggard is far more important than McQueen, so Haggard's walking about free, living in a luxury flat, and laughing.'

Craig no longer tried to argue. There was no point in arguing with a man as obsessed as Miller had become: obsessed to the point where he disdained logic.

They left the room in which the unmoving McQueen lay and returned to their car. Miller spoke as he sat down behind the wheel. 'We'll go along and have a word with Haggard.'

'D'you think that's wise right now?'

'I said, we'll have a word with Haggard.'

Miller drove at speed to Whiteacres Court. He parked the car in the forecourt and led the way to the lift.

When they reached the fifth floor, Miller knocked on the door of flat 5A. It was opened by Florence. 'He ain't in,' she said.

'We're in no hurry. We'll wait.' Miller put his foot between door and jamb.

'Get out.'

Miller pushed the door open and stepped inside. She cursed them.

'He's gone out,' she said.

'Where? To do another job? To smash up another guard?'

'He didn't do that wages job.'

'It wasn't the archangel Gabriel.'

'You'll never land him for it.'

'We'll try.'

'You'll try, all right. You never let alone. A bloke gets a bit of form so when you don't get nowhere you try and land him for it. He didn't do it.'

'Where was he on Friday morning?'

'I ain't saying nothing.'

'Hasn't he yet decided what alibi to fake? He said before he was in bed with you—doin' what? Playing mah-jongg? Or maybe he was out with Ringo Grant, studying citizen welfare?'

'I ain't saying nothing.'

'Where's he now?'

'I don't know.'

'Is he with another woman?'

She shouted a few obscenities.

'He won't keep you on for long, you know that, don't you? He'll come back with another woman and you'll be thrown out like a bit of rubbish. If you give us a bit of help now, we'll go easy on you when you're back on your turf.'

She cursed Miller.

'I'm going to search this flat,' he said. He looked at Craig and indicated with a quick nod of his head that Craig, by fair means or foul, was to keep the woman in the hall. Miller opened the door on his right and went into the room.

Craig stared at Florence, thought how strangely pure she looked, and found himself wondering what had first put her on the road she had taken. Angrily, he told himself that this was neither the time nor the place to start an enquiry into the causes of prostitution. Miller was searching the flat without any warrant or any reason to think he would find incriminating evidence, which was the act of a fool—or of a man who had allowed anger and hate completely to obscure his judgement. Haggard would cause trouble when he heard what had happened because, like all clever villains, he had discovered that he could use the law just as successfully as the innocent man.

Miller came out of the front room and went into a second one. Craig felt the sweat pin-prick his back. He'd grown to like Miller and he hated to be standing there, knowing the dangerous position Miller had placed himself in. Why couldn't he understand that a policeman was the handservant of the law, not the law itself?

Miller came out of the second room and went into a third. Florence stood quite still in the centre of the hall, hands hanging down by her sides.

Craig heard nothing to mark Haggard's arrival until the key was put in the lock of the door. 'Dusty,' he called out urgently.

Haggard entered the flat, a parcel in his right hand. When he saw Craig, his anger flared up.

'There's another in our bedroom,' said Florence shrilly.

Haggard looked across at the third door as it opened and Miller came out of the room. 'D'you let them in?' he asked harshly.

'They forced their way in. They've been threatening me, telling me what they'll do to me if I don't tell them lies.'

Haggard faced Miller. 'Let's see your search warrant.'

Miller shook his head.

'You ain't got one?'

'That's right.'

'I'll get you. You splits think you can ride anyone who's been inside, but you bloody can't. I'll get you.'

'You won't,' replied Miller.

'Want to bet on it?'

'I never bet on certainties.' Miller slowly put his right hand in his pocket, withdrew it even more slowly. There was a smile of complete satisfaction on his face. In his hand was a cotton glove. 'Remember this? It was in the pocket of one of your trousers.'

Haggard was puzzled. For the moment, he did not recognise that glove.

'We found the other of the pair by the abandoned Jaguar in Gresham car-park. There was blood on that glove which the scientists have identified as McQueen's blood. It's amazing what the scientists can do these days, isn't it? They can even make a glove talk and put a man inside on a nice long P.D. stretch.'

Haggard's memory abruptly recalled the scene as he had stuffed the gloves into his pocket. He felt utterly flabbergasted. A lousy pair of gloves, worn to prevent finger-prints, were going to send him to the nick. His anger intensified. He wanted to smash something. He wanted to get his huge hands on the detective's neck and throttle the life out of him. Had there been only one of them, he might have done just that.

· · · · ·

Reginald Breen sweated as he climbed the stairs to the first floor of Frindhurst central police station. He stopped at the head of the stairs to wipe some of the sweat from his forehead with his handkerchief. The uniformed inspector also came to a halt.

'By God, it's hot!' said Breen.

'It certainly is, sir. Good for the holiday trade.' As did most of the men, the inspector respected Breen because he was known as a genuine friend of the police force.

'But it's not good for policemen on duty in a stuffy station, eh?' Breen smiled. He replaced his handkerchief and moved forward. The inspector knocked on the chief constable's door and opened it. Breen went inside and the inspector closed the door.

Inside the room, Breen went over and sat down in one of the comfortable arm-chairs. 'I've come to tell you what I think of your police force, Charles. They've done a damn' fine job in the wages robbery and I hope you'll let them know it.'

'I certainly will. May I use your name?'

'You can say that the entire Watch Committee is very proud of them. And don't you go getting bashful over it.'

Radamski smiled. He pulled a sheet of paper closer to himself. 'We've just had one of the final reports through. Although the gloves are manufactured by the thousand and there's nothing to prove the two we've got were sold as a pair, the experts have managed to match some dirt and grease on the second glove exactly with a patch of dirt and grease on the lead-filled cosh that was used to bludgeon McQueen.'

'So there can't be the slightest doubt?'

'Not so much as the sniff of a doubt. We've got Haggard and Grant.'

'But not the other two you're certain were in on the robbery?'

'That's the one infuriating thing. Up to date, we just can't tie them in.'

'You will, Charles, and anyway, Haggard was the man you really wanted.'

'He's the brains of the outfit.' Radamski leaned back in his chair. 'The two men from R.C.S. did a lot to break the case.'

'Possibly, Charles, possibly, but they won't have done anything your chaps wouldn't have done. I told you just now not to get modest about things. Your lads did the real work and that's what matters.' Breen brought his pigskin cigarette case from his pocket and offered it. 'I'd like you to come and have lunch with me, Charles—could you manage that?'

'I certainly can, with pleasure.'

'Excellent. This is a red-letter day for the force, Charles, and I'd like to know what the London bureaucrats have to say about the kind of efficiency we've just shown.'

9

PERCY TRING had been a practising solicitor for thirty-five years. In all that time, he had had only two holidays, both taken after a monumental amount of nagging from his wife. After the second holiday, his wife left him. He was a small, balding, swarthy man with a beaked nose.

Tring looked at Haggard across the table of the interview room of Frindhurst prison.

'Well?' demanded Haggard.

Tring waited until the warder had shut the door behind himself. 'They've got a case,' he said, in his strangely toneless voice.

'I bloody well know they've got a case. Haven't they just put me up before the beaks? What kind of a case is it?'

Tring was unperturbed by the other's belligerence. 'The prosecution's case at the preliminary hearing was a very strong one.'

'All right, so it's as strong as the Bank of England. Break it. Get me off.'

'I can do my best, but no more than that.'

'You're the original optimist. What's the matter? Cold feet already? If you don't feel you can do anything, say so and I'll find someone else who can.'

'By all means,' replied Tring. He began to collect together his papers.

Haggard stared at him. 'You can't leave me now.'

'Why not?'

'But I . . . I need a mouthpiece.'

'Surely you've just declared your intention of consulting some other solicitor?'

For once, Haggard recognised the need to control himself. 'Look . . . I'm all edgy: I feel as if my mind was going to explode. When the law gets its hooks into you, it tramples you in the guts. Hang on, Mr. Tring.'

Tring dropped the papers he had been holding on to his brief-case, joined his finger tips together, and rested his elbows on the table. He waited.

'I've got to get off,' said Haggard.

'The prosecution case is a very strong one.'

'I know bleeding well . . . Look. I've got form, plenty of it. You know that. The last time I was sent down, they said I was lucky not to get seven years' P.D.'

'I would say you were exceptionally lucky.'

'They're not going to go easy this time, are they?'

'It could be as high as ten years.'

'Gawd! I can't do ten years. That much bird ends a bloke up twittering.'

'The guard was very badly injured and the medical prognosis is extremely pessimistic.'

'But the silly bastard went on fighting.'

'It was his job to fight.'

'All right, so it was his job. My job was to get the money. Why should I land ten years just for that?'

'Questions of morality are always two-sided ones.'

'And I'm always on the far side.' Haggard slammed his fist down on the table. 'You've got to get me off.'

Tring lowered his hands. 'I regret that if I am to be honest, I can offer you no hope.'

'But there's always hope.'

'A very comforting thought for those who don't wish to face the truth.'

Haggard leaned forward until his chest pressed against the table. 'What's the evidence really like?'

'In one word?'

'Yeah.'

'Overwhelming.'

'Your first name wouldn't be Job, would it?'

'It is Percival. I understood you wanted to be told the truth.'

'All right, all right, let's get a bit more truth. What are the chances of twisting the evidence?'

'I am sorry, that is not the kind of question I can discuss.'

'Why not?'

'Would you understand the meaning of the word "ethics"?'

'Of course I bleeding well . . . Listen. Ethics can be bought.'

'Even allowing so pessimistic an opinion of human nature, the price would be excessive.'

'What's excessive mean?'

'That which exceeds.'

'What price? What's the figure? What'll it take to twist the evidence?'

'I've already said . . .'

'Five hundred quid.'

'I beg your pardon?'

'Five hundred quid and it's yours to get me off.'

Tring raised one eyebrow very slightly. 'Would it be pure coincidence that this is exactly the sum the police claim you offered them as a bribe?'

'What's it signify?'

'It's merely that I have an enquiring mind.'

'Will you do it for five hundred?'

'I fear, Haggard, that you have no real conception of the seriousness of the position in which you find yourself.'

'Listen, mate, I know more about that than you do.'

'I am glad to hear it.'

'All right, all right, so I'm in a fix and you're laughing. How much d'you want to get me out of it?'

'I am forced to admit that you clearly don't believe in pleading your own cause very tactfully.'

'There ain't no cause for tact when ten years' P.D. is tapping me on the shoulder.'

Tring began to read one of his papers.

Haggard, unable to remain silent for long, demanded to know what was going to happen. He was ignored. He swore crudely and violently.

Tring turned over the sheet of paper and read the other side. He made a note in pencil and then looked up. 'It's true to say that the evidence is only overwhelmingly in favour of the prosecution at one point.'

'What's that news supposed to do to me?'

'The remaining evidence is highly suggestive, very highly suggestive, but it can do no more in a court of law than suggest and confirm what has already been proved beyond any doubt. The full force of all this evidence would not be enough in its own right to secure conviction.'

Haggard stared at him with suddenly aroused hope. 'You could do it, then?'

'Three thousand pounds, Mr. Haggard.'

Haggard looked quite bewildered.

'In addition, all expenses to be paid by you, direct.'

'Three grand?'

'Three thousand pounds.'

'You're joking.'

'I seldom joke.'

'There ain't that sort of money in the world.'

'On the contrary. The robbery netted over thirty-three thousand pounds, a very considerable proportion of which will have been profit.'

'You bleeding robber,' muttered Haggard.

* * * * *

Frindhurst assize court was small, airless, and lightless. Built in the late nineteenth century, its style was ghastly Gothic. Junior judges tended to be sent to try the cases there.

The trial of Haggard and Grant proceeded smoothly. The evidence was certain and prosecuting counsel had a great deal of experience so that he knew exactly at what level to pitch his case.

By the time Miller's examination-in-chief had been completed, no one doubted the outcome of the trial: no one, that was, except defence counsel, who had been presented with evidence which he had no cause to disbelieve, Tring, and Haggard.

Engels, defence silk, opened his cross-examination. 'Sergeant

Miller, you have given your evidence very succinctly and, if I may say so, very fairly.' Engels was a small, round man with a large stomach which he often patted, as if proud of it. He wore spectacles, but quite often held them at arm's length and used them to stab the air as he made some vital point.

Miller made no reply to this praise.

'You have very fairly, but quite rightly, admitted that when you made your way into the accused's flat on the last occasion you had no search warrant?'

'I had no warrant, sir, but Miss Jones invited both of us in.'

'Would you really think the word "invited" is the correct one? Please don't misunderstand me, however, I'm not suggesting you fought your way into the flat.'

'She did not refuse us entry, sir.'

'Your entry was pacific and to all intents and purposes unopposed?'

'Yes, sir.'

'Was the object of your visit to carry out a search?'

'There was no object, sir. Once inside, however, it seemed to me reasonable to conduct a search.'

'I expect the thought of a search had occurred to you before, though?'

'I don't think so, sir.'

'No? Well, no matter.' Engels put on his spectacles and picked up a proof, which he read. He leaned back and spoke quickly to his junior.

One of the jury was seized with a sudden fit of coughing and had to cover his mouth with a handkerchief. In the witness-box, Miller rubbed his crooked nose with his forefinger.

'Yes, Mr. Engels,' said the judge impatiently.

'I'm sorry, my Lord.' Engels stood upright and hooked his thumbs in the pockets of his frock waistcoat. 'Sergeant, I want to ask you one or two general questions. Have you at any time interviewed the driver of the armoured van?'

'Yes, sir.'

'Were you able to judge how badly injured he was?'

'Only as a layman, sir.'

'Quite so, and very neatly put. However, let me assure you

that I am not trying to trip you up on your medical knowledge. As a layman, Sergeant, you must have realised the driver was badly knocked about?'

'Yes.'

'This brutality is a terrible thing, isn't it? A kind of social cancer?'

'Yes, sir.'

'I'm sure every man and woman in court would agree. Did you see the injured guard McQueen?'

'Yes, sir.'

'You must have seen him in hospital?'

'I did.'

'More than once?'

'Twice.'

'He must present a pitiful sight?'

'Yes, sir.'

The judge intervened. 'Mr. Engels, is this evidence really relevant?'

'I venture to suggest it is, my Lord.'

'How?'

'I trust to make that clear very shortly.'

'Very well.'

Engels addressed Miller once more. 'What did you understand McQueen's condition to be after your first visit to the hospital?'

'He had not regained consciousness and would be operated on.'

'Did you gain any impression as to whether the prognosis for the operation was a good one?'

'I was told it was not.'

'Did you know before your second visit roughly what the result of the operation had been?'

'I had been told, yes, sir.'

'What had you been told?'

'That McQueen was no better.'

'When you reached the hospital, did you speak to anyone about the injured McQueen?'

'Yes.'

'To whom did you speak?'
'A sister.'
'Would this be Sister Frame?'
'Yes, sir.'
'Was this before or after you saw McQueen?'
'Before, sir.'
'What did she tell you?'
'She said that McQueen had not recovered consciousness.'
'You are telling us that you knew before you went to the hospital that he was no better and further that before you went into the room it was confirmed to you that the unfortunate man lay quite unconscious in his bed, a human cabbage?'
'Yes.'
'Then why did you, in company with Detective Constable Craig, go to the hospital at all and once there enter McQueen's room?'
'Why?'
'That's what I'm asking.'
'I don't understand.'
'I'll try to explain. On your own admission, you knew McQueen was totally unconscious and therefore quite unable to help you in any way with your enquiries. Knowing that, why did you visit him?'
'I . . . I just did.'
'Did you just do this because you were determined to refuel your hatred for the perpetrators of the crime?'
'No, sir.'
'Did you think that by staring at the man who'd been battered into a living death you would, as it were, rededicate yourself to hunting down the guilty?'
'Of course not.'
'Sergeant, were you in favour of capital punishment before it was abolished?'
Prosecuting counsel stood up. 'Really, my Lord, this is hardly a proper question.'
'Mr. Engels?' said the judge.
'My Lord, it will very soon become clear that this is not only a right and proper question, it is also a very necessary one.'

'Very well, I shall allow it.'

Once prosecuting counsel had sat down, Engels put the question again.

'I don't think it should have been abolished,' said Miller harshly.

'This is a sincere opinion, of course, and we must respect it as such. You feel that in some cases the punishment really ought to be made to fit the crime?'

'Yes.'

'Sergeant, was there much evidence against my clients at the time of your second visit to the hospital?'

'Quite a lot.'

'But at this point could either of them have been charged with the robbery?'

'No.'

'Because although you would say there was quite a lot of evidence against them, there wasn't enough?'

'Yes, sir.'

'There was not enough evidence.' Counsel put his hands on his hips. His voice became loud and harsh. 'Does this, then, explain why you dared to take the law into your own hands?'

'What . . . what d'you mean?'

'I mean that you were and are a man obsessed by the warped desire to bring to justice those whom you believed to have carried out this robbery. You, Sergeant, faked the evidence.'

'I . . . I what?' Miller gripped the edge of the box with hands that became white at the knuckles.

'You bought a pair of gloves, of the same make as the glove found by the abandoned Jaguar, and you matched the one in the police's hands. You smeared this second glove with grease and dirt from the lead-filled cosh used in the robbery, held at central police station where you worked.'

'It's a lie. It's all a lie,' shouted Miller.

Counsel continued speaking as if there had been no interruption. 'You visited the unconscious McQueen in hospital a second time in order emotionally to prepare yourself for what you were going to do and then you went to Haggard's flat when you knew Haggard was not there. You forced your way into the flat and once inside went, alone of course, into the bedroom. On your return from the bedroom you produced this glove and claimed to have found it. You faked this vital piece of evidence. You have set yourself up as judge and jury in this case.'

. . . . .

Carpenter, a witness for the defence, had features which suggested a ferret's. He had creamy white hair, beady eyes, and a thin, pointed nose which sometimes seemed to twitch. He owned a clothing shop in South Frindhurst.

'I served him myself, like. He came in and said had we got any gardening gloves. I tried to sell him some nice ones but he said he wanted gloves made by Keelers. I told him they weren't near as good as the others I'd got and there was hardly any difference in price, but he wasn't listening. Didn't seem to want to listen. So, I asks him what size he wants and he tells me large. I have one look at his hands and tells him I can see he doesn't want large or else there'll be room for both his hands in one glove. He doesn't listen to me any more than last time, but says he wants large. Got quite angry, he did. I sold him the pair. No skin off my nose, I thought.

'Then I saw his photo in the papers and it said he was the bloke what found the glove in this other bloke's pocket. I got to wondering why he'd bought a glove that didn't fit and after a bit I had a word with his lawyer.'

'Will you have a look at this glove, please.'

The glove was handed to him.

'Will you tell us if there is any distinguishing mark on this glove which would show whether it was the one you sold to Sergeant Miller.' Defence counsel addressed the Bench. 'Exhibit number seventeen, my Lord, already proved to be the glove Sergeant Miller claims to have found in the pocket of the accused's trousers.'

The judge nodded. Counsel turned round and faced the witness once more.

Carpenter examined the glove. He opened it up so that he could look inside the cuff. 'It's got a pencil mark inside.'

'Isn't it a usual thing for retailers to make a mark in the goods they sell?'

'Often happens. You can shove the price in, like, in a kind of code, or leave a mark so as if someone pinches it you can say it was yours.'

'What kind of mark is in this glove?'

'Just a small cross.'

'Can you be certain beyond all doubt you made that mark? Please be quite frank with the court. Can you swear you made that mark and there is absolutely no chance anyone else could have made it?'

'Well, it's like this, see. I mark my gloves like this and I'm sure I made this mark so as it's the glove I sold to the detective. But I suppose as it's just a small cross, someone else might do the same sort of thing.'

'Despite all other possibilities, you are sure you made this mark?'

'Yes.'

'Thank you, Mr. Carpenter.'

. . . . .

The judge turned over a page of his notebook. 'Members of the jury, you have now to consider the evidence pertaining to the finding of the glove. You will decide whether the defence allegation that Detective Sergeant Miller deliberately hid that glove in the prisoner's trouser pocket is correct. If you decide the allegation is false, you will go on to consider all the evidence on its own merits. If you decide the allegation is true, you will then very carefully ignore all evidence pertaining to the glove and will reach your decision on the remaining evidence. If you cannot reach a firm decision, you will remember that doubt must be resolved in the accuseds' favour.

'You have heard the witness, Carpenter, testify that Detective Sergeant Miller came into his shop and asked for a pair of gardening gloves made by Keelers, even though the witness advised against this make and recommended another: you have heard that the witness advised a smaller size of glove. You will remember that the glove found by the abandoned Jaguar was a large size. Prosecuting counsel was quite unable to challenge the witness's evidence at any point. Detective Sergeant Miller denies absolutely that he has ever entered Mr. Carpenter's shop and bought a pair of gloves there. Therefore you, the jury, have to decide which of those two men you believe. One is telling the truth, one is lying. To help you decide which man is lying, it is right that you should consider Sergeant Miller's attitude to this brutally carried-out crime. You will remember his own admission that he visited the hospital when he knew the guard, McQueen, was unconscious and quite unable to help the investigations. You will ask yourselves what reasonable explanation there can be for this visit, if not the one that defence counsel claims. You have heard Detective Sergeant Miller express his hatred—that is not, I suggest, too strong a word—of men who so violently break the law. You may agree with defence counsel that his personal feelings in this case were far stronger than was right and proper . . .'

·   ·   ·   ·   ·

The foreman of the jury had a large, florid face and a handlebar moustache.

'Have you reached your verdict and is it the verdict of you all?' asked the clerk of the court.

'We have. Not guilty.'

10

DETECTIVE SUPERINTENDENT WATTERS travelled from London to Frindhurst by train. Head of the section of R.C.S. under which Miller served, he was a taciturn Scot with a name for a driving ambition that, it was said, would either eventually ruin him or lead him to the top of his profession.

Craig met him at the railway station and drove him to the central police station. Watters did not speak throughout the journey and on their arrival he confined himself to saying he would be catching the four-eighteen train back to London and where was the chief constable's office? Back in the R.C.S. room, Craig found Miller sitting at his desk, trying to make out he was working.

Miller looked up. 'Has . . . has he come?'

'I've just delivered him.'

'They say he's sharper than a needle?'

'He's got about as many manners: found it difficult even to say good afternoon.' Craig was embarrassed by the knowledge of the trouble Miller was in. What was going to be the upshot of it? Dismissal from the force and a trial for perjury? A policeman found guilty of perjury could expect no mercy from the courts, no matter what were the forces that drove him to commit that perjury.

Miller picked up a pencil and fiddled with it. 'I wonder at what stage I'll get called in?'

Craig said the obvious thing, that he didn't know. Miller was now a man who knew only despair. Craig wondered whether Violet Miller had somehow managed to remain cheerful in the face of all that had happened.

The telephone rang and Miller lifted the receiver. He listened for several seconds, said 'Yes, sir,' and replaced the receiver. He stood up. 'The royal summons.' He left the room, walking very slowly as if he had suddenly grown old.

Craig opened up the departmental memoranda file and began to file the latest plethora of communications from H.Q. At times, the police force seemed to have become one vast bureaucratic machine, dedicated to using up more and more time of more and more highly trained policemen: no beat in the county was fully manned and perhaps the most powerful single reason for this was the number of men whose time was taken up in office work.

He looked at his watch. Dusty had been gone over a quarter of an hour now. Could he hope to escape dismissal from the force? The bloody fool, thought Craig angrily.

He lit a cigarette. Violet Miller had had such a pride in her husband's part in the police force: where was that pride now?

He checked on the time again. Half an hour. Was Miller still in there, facing the chief constable and Watters? Watters looked as if he could be really mean.

Three-fifty-five p.m. and time to find Watters and take him to the station to catch the four-eighteen train back to London. Craig left and went along the short stretch of corridor to the chief constable's room. He knocked on the door and entered.

The chief constable, in very smart uniform, was sitting behind the desk and Watters, in sloppy suit, was sitting in front of it. Miller was not there.

'It's time to leave, sir,' said Craig.

'Mr. Watters will be down to the car in a moment,' said the chief constable.

Craig left and went down the stairs, along the corridor separating the courtroom from the police station, and out into the courtyard.

One of the patrol cars had just driven in and the two uniformed constables were standing by it, checking through their log book. The elder of the two spoke.

'What's the verdict?'

'I don't know.'

'Haven't they yet . . .' The speaker became silent as he saw Watters come out of the doorway, accompanied by the duty inspector.

Watters sat down in the passenger seat. 'This car's seen enough service,' he said, as Craig got in behind the wheel.

'Yes, sir. I think it was handed on from the driving school.'

'Better equipment will be through before the year's out.'

They drove out of the courtyard and on to the road. At the end of Foostey Road there was a queue of six cars, waiting to turn right into Station Road.

The detective superintendent sat silent until the queue of cars had dispersed and the police car was going up Station Road. 'You'll be on your own until I can send someone elese down.'

'Yes, sir.' So that's the end of Dusty, thought Craig bitterly.

'In the meantime, you'll seek any assistance you need from the borough police and you'll report to Detective Chief Inspector Barnard. Is that clear?'

'Yes, sir.'

Immediately before the railway bridge, they turned into the parking area. Craig climbed out and began to go round the car to see Watters out of it, but the other was already standing on the road.

'Craig,' said Watters.

'Sir?'

'If you've any sense, you'll have learned a very important lesson. Goodbye.' Watters turned and went across to the stairs which led up to the booking-hall that straddled the railway lines.

That night, Craig's supper was a soggy mass of baked beans on two slices of soggy toast and a portion of jam roly-poly, slimy on the outside. When he left the roly-poly, his sharp voiced landlady demanded to know if he was calling her cooking no good? Accepting the part of a coward, he said that her cooking was delicious, but that he was not feeling very well. She replied that she hoped he was not sickening for the 'flu, or anything like that, because her house was a nice clean house and she wanted to keep it that way.

A quarter of an hour after the meal, he left the house and walked along the roads. The evening was warm and windless and, despite the depressing houses on either side which looked like an endless row of rabbit hutches, the walk was a pleasant one. He took no deliberate course and was surprised after twenty minutes to find himself in the road in which the Millers were living.

He wondered whether he ought to go and see them, almost persuaded himself that at a time like the present they would far rather be on their own when his conscience intervened to say that if he was determined to avoid the meeting he should admit the fact to himself. He went along to their house and knocked on the door. The owner of the house, a small, cheerful, bird of a woman opened the door for him. He went through to the sitting-room.

Only Miller and his wife were in the room. Violet Miller was sitting with some knitting in her hands but making no effort to knit, and Miller was standing by the window and staring blankly at the road.

They turned and looked at him as he entered. 'Hullo, John,' she said in a dull voice.

'I thought . . . Just called in.'

'Sit down and I'll get some coffee.' She put the knitting on the arm of the chair, stood up, looked at her husband and seemed about to say something, then left the room.

Miller walked to the sofa and sat down. His face looked slack and lined. 'I'm sorry I couldn't come back this afternoon to let you know what was happening.'

'That's all right,' replied Craig, aware how trite the remark was.

'I didn't feel I could face it.'

'What . . . what did the super say?'

'Not much, but enough. There'll be a police investigation and if they can't find anything to disprove the evidence given against me in court I'll be up for perjury.'

'Maybe . . .' began Craig, but became silent.

'How the hell can they hope to prove the bastard was lying?'

'If only . . .' Again Craig stopped.

'If only what?'

'If only you'd waited a bit, we'd probably eventually have found the evidence we needed,' said Craig, miserably aware that these were no words of comfort.

Shocked, Miller stared at him. 'What d'you mean?' His voice was high.

'We could have landed them some other way.'

Miller stood up. 'Are you saying you think I planted that glove?'

Craig did not answer.

'God Almighty, don't you know me any better than the rest of the fools?'

Violet Miller hurried back into the room. 'Albert, what's the matter?'

'Matter? I'll tell you what the matter is. John is certain I planted the glove. I told you the whole bloody world believes I did.'

'Oh, John!' she said.

'But . . .' began Craig.

'How could you believe that?'

'But Dusty was always cursing because we couldn't land Haggard. Look how he said time after time that the law's too soft and a policeman can't get anywhere if he keeps to the book.'

'And that automatically makes me guilty?' demanded Miller.

'Why did you take me to the hospital just before we went to Haggard's flat? Why did we go to Haggard's flat?'

Miller lit a cigarette with fingers that shook. His voice was hoarse. 'I'm doing my last two years in the force, to average up my pay for a bigger pension. D'you think I'm going out of my way to muck up that pension? Do you? If the law's soft, that's the law's fault: if people get hurt, let 'em shout at the law. All right, I know I cursed like mad when I saw McQueen nearly battered to death: all right, so I hate the bastards who did it. But d'you think I'm going to go out on a mile-long limb just to make certain the guilty men are found guilty and imprisoned? My pension's more important to me than that. To hell with anything that mucks up my pension. I've a wife to support, and kids to finish bringing up. D'you really imagine I'd toss their fortune away just to get Haggard to court? I hate Haggard, but I love my family far more. If we'd never landed him I'd have gone on cursing, but I'd never have been fool enough to manufacture evidence. Give me credit for some common sense.'

'I . . . It seemed so certain,' said Craig weakly.

'So I noticed.'

'What are you going to do?'

'Prove he's innocent,' said Violet.

Miller turned and faced her. He gesticulated with his hands. 'I'm going to prove my innocence, oh, yes!, but how?' He spoke to Craig again. 'All the time, that one word goes tearing through my mind: how? Carpenter lied on oath, so he's not going to willingly admit to perjury. Then how do I prove all the negatives: that I was never in that shop, that I didn't plant the glove when I was on my own in the bedroom, that I didn't wipe the glove on the cosh beforehand? You tell me how I go about proving all those things didn't happen?'

Craig was silent.

'That's just about it,' said Miller.

'Carpenter identified the mark on the glove,' said Craig.

'Still not ready to believe me?'

'It's not that, Dusty, I'm just thinking as other people'll think.'

'You're good at that, aren't you? All right, I'll tell you what to say to all the nice charitable people. Carpenter had his original story ready and told it. The defence lapped it up and forced the authorities to show Carpenter the glove. He noticed this mark inside and was quick enough and smart enough to see how he could make use of it. It was the kind of mark a hundred and one shopkeepers must make.'

'Why should Carpenter be lying?' asked Violet Miller frantically.

'Because he was paid enough to make it worth while.'

'Then the police must be able to find that out, Albert. They must be able to trace all the money he was paid.'

'Perhaps.'

'But they must, Albert.'

Miller stubbed out his cigarette and sat down. 'I know one thing. They'll break their backs in search of the truth.' He lit another cigarette. 'I've been having nightmares, wondering what could happen if the truth never came out. But it must.' He looked across at his wife and smiled for the first time for a very long while. 'Let's all go out to the local and wet our whistles and drink to the boys in blue. May they clear the whole thing up in a brace of shakes.'

11

RADAMSKI and his wife had been asked to dine with the Breens. They dressed with care and timed their drive to bring them to the Breens' house ten minutes after the time stated, as social custom dictated.

The four of them drank a bottle of Heidseick before the meal and a bottle of Richebourg, *Domaine de la Romanée-Conti*, with the main course. After finishing the dessert, the ladies retired. Breen put a decanter of port on the table, together with a box of Coronas. He waited until Radamski had filled his glass with port and then pushed the cigars across the table together with a cutter. Radamski cut off the end of a cigar and lit it with a Swan Vestas match. He sipped the port. 'This is really good,' he said.

Breen was pleased by the appreciation. 'How about guessing what it is, Charles?'

'Good heavens, no. My father was a connoisseur, but ever since I've taken an interest in it it's been far too expensive for me to learn much about it.'

'Cockburn, twenty-seven. I bought ten dozen just after the war when the Hampton estate was sold.'

Radamski thought that for Breen to bring out so treasured a nectar, he must be wanting something pretty big.

Breen gave himself port and a cigar. He settled back in his chair. 'It's nice to meet someone like you, Charles, who knows enough of what's good in life to enjoy it. That means quite a bit to the position you hold. There's no point to our having a graceless chief constable: look at the people he has to meet and how many of those see him as a representative of the town.

I don't mind telling you now that when we were making the appointment we took a great deal into consideration that weren't strictly police matters. Frindhurst has an image and it's an image well worth keeping. You'd agree with that, now you've been here a while?'

'I most certainly would.'

'Henry Ford is reputed to have said that history is bunk, but if so it shows he didn't know much outside of how to build cars cheaply. History isn't bunk: it's the blood that brings life to the arteries of the country. When a bit of history dies or is lost, the arteries lose some of their life-force.' He carefully passed the decanter of port across.

Radamski refilled his glass.

'This town represents a lot, Charles, a lot that's strong and a hundred per cent worth while. During the last war, a greater proportion of the town's men were in the armed forces than of any other town in the British Isles. I don't suppose you knew that?'

'No, I didn't.'

'History, tradition, and they're two facets of the same thing, really counts. In a very short space of time, you've brought a true sense of tradition to the borough police force.'

'I hope I have.'

'I know you have. What's more, in those few years you've raised its standards until it doesn't have to take second place to any other force in the country. How does your clear-up rate compare with the national level?'

'Quite a bit higher.'

'Stop being modest, Charles. Is there a force with a better rate?'

'Actually, I don't know of one.'

'Precisely. And yet this is the force they want to do away with. We had to accept the Regional Crime Squad because if we didn't the Home Secretary was going to withdraw his fifty per cent grant and leave us quite unable to operate any force at all, but we're not just tamely going to let them come along and absorb our force into a national one, with all the attendant dangers. I know you're with me in this?'

'I couldn't agree more.'

Breen refilled his glass. He sipped the port slowly, savouring each mouthful. 'Sergeant Miller's actions have hardly brought credit to the Regional Crime Squad.'

'Unfortunately, they've rebounded to the discredit of the police in general.'

'I'm not concerned with the police in general.'

Radamski was silent.

'A thing like a national police force can only take hold if it remains healthy. That's one of the elementary laws of nature. A parasite only overcomes its host when it's potentially stronger: cut out a cancer before it gains strength and you save the parent body. What's going to happen if Miller is found guilty of perjury?'

Radamski held his glass by the stem and slowly twisted it round, watching the subtle play of colour as the port caught the light. 'Illogically, since it's entirely the fault of the man and not the system, it's almost inevitable that the system will be blamed.'

'And R.C.S. will have started life with its face very nastily smeared.' Breen leaned forward and his voice quickened. 'If its first operation in this town ends in catastrophe, it's not ever going to find the strength to take over its host, is it?'

'I wouldn't have thought so.'

Breen finished his port. 'There'll have to be a very careful investigation.'

Radamski chose his words carefully. 'We have already been asked to carry it out.'

'R.C.S. could hardly carry it out themselves. You won't be afraid to publish the truth, will you? In a matter like this, the truth is the most important thing there is.'

'If Miller went that far beyond the boundaries of his duties, I certainly shan't try to hush up the matter in any way for the sake of the general image of the police.'

Breen poured himself another port. 'Presumably, you'll take direct charge of investigations?'

'I'm sure that will be the best.'

They drank and smoked in silence for several minutes, each

immersed in his own thoughts. The 365-day clock on the marble mantelpiece chimed the half-hour. Out in the hall, the grandfather clock chimed only seconds later.

'I suppose we'd better go and join our wives,' said Breen. He stood up.

* * * * *

Haggard was sprawled out in the arm-chair. On the table by his side was a bottle of whisky, a soda syphon, and a glass. Opposite him, on the settee, sat Florence. She was nervous.

'Why didn't you stay out there on your turf?' he demanded, as insultingly as possible. 'Why come back here?'

'I only went back because you were inside, Tom. I had to get money from somewhere.'

'You lying bitch.'

'I'm not lying, I swear I'm not.' There was a note of desperation in her voice. 'Didn't I come back here the moment they let you go?'

'You came back. I'm asking why?'

'Why? . . . I don't understand.'

'No one asked you.'

'Please, please, you know why I came.'

He finished his drink and poured himself another.

'I had to go back out to work,' she said. 'You didn't leave me any money.'

'Leave you any money? Why should I?'

'I just meant——'

'I don't owe you anything, do I?'

'Of course not.'

'Then why should I leave you money?'

'But I'm not saying you ought, I'm only trying to tell you why I had to go back to work. I swear I didn't want to go.'

'Turn the record off.'

'But you said——'

'I said this flat's too crowded. You're always moaning and groaning: makes like the flat's got a Cassandra in it.'

'Cassandra?'

'You ignorant bitch,' he said scornfully.

She left the sofa and came and knelt by his side. She began to fondle him. He gripped her arm and twisted, so that she crashed to the floor. Her skirt rode up her legs and Haggard, who had been in prison for several weeks, was unable to ignore the sight.

She lay as she had fallen. 'I knew you'd get off,' she whispered.

'Yeah? Is that why you were in such a hurry to leave when they put me in the nick?'

'You're so clever. No one else could have got off.'

He drank heavily.

She curled round, careful not to move her skirt down, and gripped his legs as she pressed herself against them. 'I love you, Tom. Oh God, I love you!'

He moved his right toe until he could press it into her side. He saw her flinch heavily, but she did not cry out and she did not let go of him. He suffered an emotion akin to admiration. Any woman who willingly suffered as many humiliations as she did had something. Women were suckers for being humiliated. They loved being humiliated because they were all masochists to a greater or lesser extent. According to a book he'd read, women were masochists because they were conditioned willingly to bear the pain of childbirth. Could anything be stupider?

'You're really glad I'm back, aren't you?' she pleaded.

'Like hell. I'm getting ready to lay on another bit.'

'Who?' Her voice rose.

He shrugged his shoulders.

'I'll kill any brass I see you with.'

'You'll be busy killing.'

'I look after you well, don't I?'

'No one don't look after me. I look after myself.'

'Let me look after you.' She fondled him again and this time he made no attempt to stop her. 'No one's as clever as you.'

'I manage.' He was clever. He'd got off the hook and dropped a split into the mud. Detective Sergeant Miller. A worn-out, bald-headed, broken-nosed split who'd been stupid enough to turn down a five hundred pound bung. More money than he'd ever see in one piece from the police. If a man could be that stupid, he could be anything: cousin to the Queen's jester, even.

. . . . .

The following morning, Craig went along to the detective chief inspector's office. The D.C.I. was not there, but Detective Constable Nachton was.

'Where's the Guv'nor?' asked Craig.

'With his serene highness,' replied Nachton, in a loud and breezy voice. Nachton was a prominent member of the police rugby team.

'Is he going to be long?'

'Not knowing, can't say. Still, old Radswallop usually spits out what he's got to say in double quick time. Left, right, left, right, salute, about turn.'

Barnard suddenly came into the room, surprising both of them. Nachton hastily said he had just put the latest list of stolen property on the desk and left. Craig waited in silence as Barnard went round his desk and sat down.

Barnard's face was flushed, suggesting his meeting with the chief constable had hardly been an amicable one. 'Yes?'

'Could I have a word with you, sir?'

'Yes, but don't take long about it. Sit down.'

Craig sat down on one of the hard wooden seats.

'Well?'

'It's about Sergeant Miller, sir.' There was so much Craig wanted to say, but the difference in rank made it difficult for him to speak at all freely.

'Yes?'

'I saw him last night, sir. He's completely innocent. He didn't plant that glove in Haggard's trousers.'

Barnard looked across the desk and in his lugubrious expression there was a suggestion of both anger and sympathy. 'There'll be a full investigation into the matter. You know that.'

'Yes, sir. But I also know he's innocent.'

'Can you prove it?'

'Not . . . not exactly prove. But he's due to retire before very long. . . . Sir, he would never have done such a thing after so long in the force.'

'Unfortunately, he made no secret of his hatred for thugs.'

'Hatred's one thing, sir, planting evidence is another. No real policeman would plant evidence.'

'It's been known.'

'But he didn't do it.'

'Look, Craig, you know as well as I do that your opinion, and mine, are valueless and that the only thing which matters is proof. Right now it doesn't matter a hang how many of us would go bail for Miller. In court, a man on oath said Miller faked evidence and the jury believed him—or put at the very lowest, didn't disbelieve him. Now there's going to be a police enquiry into the allegations and if they're not disproved beyond all doubt Detective Sergeant Miller will stand trial for perjury.'

'Is Carpenter's bank balance going to be checked?'

'I trust I can adequately conduct this investigation without the need of any prompting from you.'

'Yes, sir. I didn't mean it like that.'

Barnard picked up the list of stolen property and looked at it. 'Have you said all you want to?' he asked harshly.

'I . . . Could I assist in the investigations, sir?'

'No.'

'I'd really like to.'

'That's all.'

Craig stood up slowly. He hesitated, then turned and left. Barnard dropped the sheet of paper on to his desk. He stared across at the far wall, on which hung maps of the borough and the county. He picked up a pencil and held it with both hands. As his expression became really bitter, he snapped the pencil.

12

ON MONDAY, the mercurial weather changed its pattern yet again. The day was overcast and a cool wind was blowing. There were few people on the beaches and the sea looked sullen and dirty. The bed-and-breakfasters wandered around the streets trying to make time pass, like lost and damned souls.

Craig sat in the R.C.S. room and stared unseeingly at a Telex message reporting a breaking and entering at Gresham. Yesterday evening he had gone to see Dusty and his wife. Dusty was trying to keep up both their spirits by constant professions of the absolute certainty of success of the police enquiries, but he could not begin to hide his fears.

Craig put down the Telex message and no longer pretended to himself he was reading it. Were the Frindhurst police doing everything possible? Were they forgetting everything else and concentrating entirely on proving the innocence of a detective sergeant who had been framed? Barnard might be sourer than vinegar, but they said he was a first-class detective. He wouldn't miss a trick and he must ferret out the truth. If only Dusty hadn't been so open in his protestations of justice at any price when that wasn't what he believed: to an outsider, he had become so emotionally involved in the case that he had faked the evidence to procure the guilt of a man who, but for the evidence, could not have been brought to trial. Yet Dusty had never begun to intend to practise what he preached.

Craig stood up. He should go over to Gresham, but that journey would have to wait. He must find out how the investigations into Dusty's innocence were getting on.

He left the room and went down the corridor and right, to the interview and C.I.D. rooms. In the C.I.D. general room the three desks were covered with papers and files, two new but damaged bicycles were propped against the far wall, one of the four cupboards was open to show it was filled from top to bottom with files, and a large pile of books had fallen, leaving books all over the uncarpeted floor. Detective Constable Nachton was filling out a crime report, laboriously typing with two forefingers. He looked up.

'What can we do for you? A couple of T forty-one forms to give you indigestion, or a leave pass for twenty-one days and a blank expense account?'

Craig sat down on the edge of the other's desk. He offered cigarettes. 'How's the case going?'

'Which one? At this precise moment we've got two class one crimes, a dozen class two, and God knows how many odds and sods.'

'Dusty.'

'Oh!' Nachton leaned back in his chair, which creaked heavily.

'Has anything turned up yet?'

'Not yet.' Nachton for once became serious. 'What's more, if you ask me nothing much will.'

'Why not?'

'Because the higher-ups are too certain of what's what to bother too hard.'

'They can't be certain.'

'Well, whatever it is, they're not killing themselves.' Nachton flicked the ash from his cigarette on to the floor. 'I went with Barnard to interview that creep Carpenter. Barnard handled him with kid gloves instead of lashing into him good and proper.'

'There must be some reason.'

'If it's not what I've already said, you name it.'

'But . . . but then why?'

'Who knows? In any case, Dusty's got himself to blame as much as anyone. He wasn't ever backward in saying how he'd fix things so that the guilty would always be punished. If that's the way you think, at least keep quiet about it.'

'It was only talk. He didn't plant the glove. Why the hell should he take such a risk when he'd be so easily found out?'

'No one ever thinks he's going to be caught. That always happens to the next bloke.'

'Dusty didn't plant the glove.'

Nachton shook his head.

Craig stepped off the desk and left the room. Why wasn't Barnard forcing the pace? What in the hell was Barnard thinking about? Perhaps he was stupid enough to believe Dusty had planted the glove, but he ought to be doing his very damnedest to prove otherwise. As Dusty hadn't planted the glove, the proof of his innocence must be around somewhere. If Barnard wasn't going to pull his fingers out, who was?

Craig returned to his room and looked down at the Telex message he had earlier read. He had to go to Gresham, but there was nothing to stop his going via South Frindhurst and Carpenter's clothing shop. Nothing, that was, except the knowledge that he would be exceeding his duty by a mile and if Barnard caught up with him he'd be poleaxed. A man didn't get sent to Bramshill or get chosen for a university course by ignoring orders. Yet, how could one match up anything against the sick look in Dusty and Violet's eyes: the look of people who were helpless because they were being overwhelmed by something completely beyond their control.

He went down the back stairs to the courtyard and drove out in the squeaking, labouring R.C.S. Humber. At the turning for Gresham, he carried straight on, to South Frindhurst.

The shop was on the corner and it sold all kinds of clothing, for men and women, mostly at what were claimed to be greatly reduced prices. Craig went in and spoke to an assistant whose hair resembled an exploding broom. He asked where Mr. Carpenter was. The assistant in a high, squeaky voice suggested he might be in the office.

The office was little more than a box-room and was almost completely filled with clothing in boxes, cartons, and loose. Carpenter sat at the small desk, head bent low over a ledger, pencil in right hand. He looked round as Craig knocked on the open door. 'Yes, what is it?'

'I'm Detective Constable Craig.'

He put the pencil down. 'Don't you people ever leave a man in peace?' He ran a hand through his creamy white hair and his beady eyes looked at Craig, flicked to the right, came back, then flicked to the left.

'I've only a few questions.'

'I've already answered enough of 'em today to fill a dictionary and the bloke what came earlier promised I wouldn't be troubled again. He was dead wrong, wasn't he?'

'It's a man's innocence at stake.'

'And my business is at stake. If I don't check everything backwards and forwards five times, my loyal assistants will do me into the bankruptcy courts. I'm not wasting any more time.'

'Can you be absolutely certain it was Sergeant Miller who bought the gloves?'

'Give over, chum. D'you think I'd've stood up in court and said what I did if I'd any doubts?'

'You might have done.'

'Now look, you don't come in me own office calling me a liar and that's straight.'

'I didn't mean it like that. It's just that eyewitness identification is very tricky at the best of times.'

'The bloke had a nose what was twisted into a corkscrew. D'you think I'm going to mistake him for Jayne Mansfield?'

'But can't you see he might have called in here for something else and not for gloves? You could have mixed him up quite unintentionally.'

'Didn't he swear at the trial he'd never come in this shop for nothing? He came in here and I served him and that's God's truth. I want some gardening gloves, he says, a pair of Keelers. I try to tell him I can sell him a much better pair for almost the same price, but he's not listening. He tells me he wants a large pair. I look at his hands and tell him he doesn't want large or he'll lose his hands inside. Large size, he says, so large size I sells him. You're nuts, I thought, until I read about the trial and realised maybe he wasn't as nuts as I'd thought.'

'Why did you serve him?'

'There ain't no law to say I shouldn't.'

'What I mean is, with those assistants in the shop to help you, do you normally serve customers?'

Carpenter rubbed the tip of his pointed nose. 'This shop's run efficient. If a customer's waiting, I serves him. I'm humble. I don't mind waiting on a customer.'

'Then Sergeant Miller was waiting around and the other assistants were busy?'

Carpenter rubbed his nose again, but did not answer.

'Why don't they remember his coming into the shop?'

'Like you've just said, they was busy.'

'Or was it because he was never here?'

'What you driving at? I ain't lying and no one's coming here and telling me I is. I served him like I said and if no one else didn't notice him, that's no skin off my nose.'

'But can't you see that his whole career's at stake?' Craig spoke urgently. 'He swears you've made a mistake. If there's the slightest chance you——'

'I said in court what I've got to say.'

'Just the vaguest possibility . . .'

'There ain't none.'

Wearily, Craig turned and walked to the door. 'How's business doing?' he asked, as he reached the doorway.

'I'm buying property on the Riviera so as to get rid of all me profits, that's how.'

Craig walked across the shop to the counter at which stood the tousle-headed assistant. 'I'd like a pair of gardening gloves. The ones made by Keelers.'

'Keelers?'

'That's right.'

The assistant reluctantly moved. He went off and searched amongst some drawers and spoke to another assistant. He came back. 'We ain't none of them.'

'D'you mean you don't stock them?'

'We ain't got none, that's all I know.'

'Thanks. Any handkerchiefs?'

'Thousands, mate. Plain or fancy?'

'Two plain white.'

The assistant served him. 'That the lot?'

'Yes, thanks.'

'A couple of bob, mate, and dear at half the price.'

Craig paid. 'I hear business is good with you?'

'Good? Who's been feeding you with that sort of news? If I gave you a quid for every customer what's been in today, you wouldn't be going out a millionaire, I can tell you. And d'you know why? The stuff they sell ain't no good, that's why.'

Unnoticed by both of them, Carpenter had left the office and come across the shop. 'You little bleeder,' he shouted at the assistant. 'Our merchandise is good.'

'Good for what, mate? Rags?'

'You're fired. D'you hear me? Fired.'

'I'm walking out, mate, first.' The assistant spoke loudly to Craig. 'Been trying to sell this place, but 'e ain't never found no one stupid enough to buy it. Me—I wouldn't 'ave it as a gift.'

An angry row developed between the two. Craig picked up the two handkerchiefs he had just bought and left. Once on the pavement, he examined them for any form of marking, such as the small cross Carpenter claimed to have put in the gloves, but there was none.

On finishing his work at Gresham, he entered up his log book to show a direct journey from Frindhurst and a stay at Gresham police station three-quarters of an hour longer than it had, in fact, been. He returned to Frindhurst and used a public call-box to telephone the banks. The third bank he spoke to said that Carpenter had an account with them. He drove to the bank and, after a short wait, saw the manager.

The manager was a small, fussy man who wanted every i dotted twice. He listened to Craig and then spoke testily. 'I don't quite understand the point of your enquiries.'

'We're investigating certain allegations that arose from the recent trial, sir.'

'Quite. I understand that clearly enough. But how can the account of one of our clients be of any concern?'

'We're pretty certain it is, sir.'

'Then please tell me what possible significance can it have?'

'We want to know if his business is prosperous, or not: whether he's in debt: whether a large sum of money was paid into his account just before the trial.'

'I told the police that no large sum of money has been paid to his name. I can't understand why you're not fully aware of that?'

Before a further five minutes were up, Craig had to admit his visit was a failure. Without greater authority than he could show, the manager was not going to produce a statement of Carpenter's accounts. He thanked the manager for his co-operation, without sounding sarcastic, and left.

As he walked along the High Street to where he had parked his car, he cursed the blanket of frustration which muffled all his efforts. What had he accomplished so far? Nothing: plain, ordinary, frustrating nothing.

. . . . .

At nine-thirty-three the following morning, Craig was called into Barnard's office and told to bring his log book with him.

'Sit down,' said Barnard. 'Let me see your log, please.'

Craig passed the book across and Barnard opened and read it. After a while he put the book, opened, down on his desk and sat back in his chair. 'Is this an accurate record?'

'Yes, sir.'

'You are quite certain?'

'Yes, sir.'

'Craig, there are two things I demand of any officer under my command, which at the moment includes you. He should never lie to me and never fail to carry out his duties. Do you understand?'

'Sir?'

'You have just lied to me. Your log book is incorrectly

made out and you know it: you also know that you have not been carrying out your duties.' Seeing Craig was about to speak, Barnard checked him. 'Before you dive even deeper into the mud, let me tell you that I've received a complaint from Mr. Carpenter. He said that twice yesterday he was troubled by the police and on the second visit the officer concerned went out of his way to be insolent and to cause trouble. Because of this officer's actions, one of the assistants left. Is that true?'

'No, sir.'

'Are you denying you visited the shop?'

'I'm denying I caused any trouble.'

'Why is there no record of your visit in your log?'

Craig did not answer.

'Why did you lie to me a moment ago when I questioned you about this visit?'

Again, Craig was silent.

'What the devil d'you think you're doing?' snapped Barnard.

'Trying to prove Miller's innocence, sir.'

'Don't be insolent.'

'I'm not . . .'

'You're very well aware that the borough police are investigating the case. It's sheer insolence to suggest that they aren't doing their job properly.'

'I never said they weren't, sir.'

Barnard started to speak angrily, then stopped. He shut the log book with a snap and pushed it across the desk. 'Your police record is a good one and I'm not going to black it because of what's happened. To some extent, I can understand and sympathise with your desire to help a colleague. But it's not your job to work on the case and if there's any suspicion of it happening again I'll report the matter on a D form. Is that quite clear?'

'Yes, sir.'

'That's all.'

Craig stood up and picked up the log book. 'Sir?'

'What?'

'I tried to buy a pair of Keelers' gardening gloves in Carpenter's store. The assistant said they didn't stock them.'

'We've already gone into that matter. Do I have to remind you that the C.I.D. are not morons?'

'I gather no one's exactly killing himself investigating.'

'Get out,' shouted Barnard.

Craig left.

13

CRAIG reached the Millers' house as they were finishing eating supper. They brushed aside his apologies for interrupting their meal with an eagerness that showed how desperately they had been waiting for him.

'Well?' demanded Miller. 'How much have you discovered?'

Craig shook his head.

Miller's expression changed abruptly from one of hope to one of tired defeat. His wife looked away so that the others should not see her face.

'Nothing at all?' muttered Miller.

'I discovered nothing. Then the D.C.I. found out what I'd been up to, had me in his room, and tore me up for confetti.'

Violet Miller turned back. 'Albert didn't do it,' she said wildly, as if constant repetition would have some effect.

Miller sat down at the table and pushed away his plate on which there was still a portion of jam tart. 'The kids have been getting it,' he said.

'How d'you mean?' asked Craig.

'Getting it at their schools. They're new there and with my case plastered all over the papers they're fair game. Ronald came back yesterday with a badly bruised face.' Miller looked up. 'It wasn't a straight fight. Nothing as equal as that for those little bastards. Three of 'em got on to him and said his dad was a crook and when he tried to argue all three of 'em beat him up. He's learned something, John, something important. You can't fight more'n you can take on.'

'You've got to go on fighting,' said his wife.

'Fight? What am I going to fight? I'm stuck. I know the

truth, but no one else is interested in that.' Miller slumped back in his chair.

Craig shifted his weight from one foot to the other.

'Sit down, John,' said Violet Miller.

He sat down. 'Would you like a beer?' she asked.

'No, thanks.'

'Please have one.'

He was about to refuse again when he realised how much she wanted him to accept.

He left the house an hour later. His last words had been to assure them both that the borough C.I.D. were moving heaven and earth to discover the truth. He hadn't had the courage to say anything else.

He walked along the pavement. He felt as if he were wading through an ever stickier sea of treacle as thick fog covered everything and only lifted tantalisingly for seconds at a time. There was, at the moment, no hope of uncovering proof of Dusty's innocence. So? Was Dusty inevitably to be disgraced, thrown to the world without his desperately desired pension because the world falsely believed that he had given them justice in an unjust manner? It couldn't happen like that. Innocence had to win in a fight against guilt. But what if there could be no fight? Haggard, utterly vicious, utterly amoral, had escaped conviction by falsely proving Miller a liar and a perjurer. If justice meant anything, he must not be allowed to get away with it.

Craig lit a cigarette. Bitterly, he thought that fine emotions were heady things but, as with liquor, when their influence was over, depression raced in. Haggard must be fought, but fought with what, where, how?

Craig visualised the luxury flat Haggard lived in and saw it as a thing rotten to the core. McQueen lay in hospital, alive in a medical sense, but no other: Dusty Miller was on the way to having his life ruined.

An idea swept Craig's mind. Suppose he spoke to Haggard and tried to persuade him to tell the truth, now that he was publicly cleared of the robbery? Might there not be some latent streak of decency in him? Craig's imagination tried to reject the idea: to speak to Haggard must be to suffer humiliation and what point was there in subjecting himself to such humiliation? He checked his imagination. Humiliation or no, he must go.

He walked to the police station, collected the creaking Humber, and drove to the luxury flats. He took the lift up to the fifth floor and knocked on the door of 5A. Florence opened the door. She was wearing a simple print dress that made her look like somebody's débutante sister.

'What d'you want?' she asked shrilly.

'A word with Haggard.'

'Who is it?' Haggard shouted from one of the rooms.

'One of the splits.' As she waited she stared fixedly at the right of Craig, as if to look directly at him would be to corrupt herself.

Haggard came into the hall. He was wearing a patterned silk shirt, open at the neck, and grey flannel trousers with knife-edge creases.

'May I have a word with you?' asked Craig.

Haggard was puzzled by so politely put a request. 'What's the form?'

'I'd like to ask you something.'

'What?'

Craig hesitated, searching for the right words. 'It's about Miller,' he said finally.

'Yeah?'

'He's been suspended from duty. He may be put on trial for perjury.'

'So?' Haggard was more puzzled than ever. He leaned forward until his weight was on the balls of his feet, as if expecting violence.

'Would . . . would you tell the truth now?'

'The truth?'

Craig spoke more rapidly. 'You got off, were found not guilty of the robbery, so it doesn't matter what happens now because they can't go for you a second time. If you admitted it was your glove, it wouldn't affect you and it would save him.'

'Save him?'

'Save him from being dismissed the force and convicted of perjury.'

'You . . . you've come here to ask me to help a split out of trouble?'

'He's married, Haggard, to a wonderful woman and he's got two children. They're just of an age when something like this could blast their lives.'

'Hold it. Just say it again, will you? You've come here to plead for him?'

'I'm asking you to tell the truth. Will you, for the sake of his family?'

'His family?'

'You'd never regret doing it.'

'I'll tell you what. You get down on your knees and beg.'

'Get down on my knees?' repeated Craig.

Looking at Craig's face, Haggard could no longer control his laughter. For a few seconds he was unable to speak, then he managed to get the words out. 'A split! Flo, d'you see him? D'you hear him? A split, prayin' to me to be nice.'

'His wife . . .' began Craig desperately.

Haggard's laughter stopped abruptly. 'You must be real simple. Help a split? I wouldn't turn round to pull a split out of a sewer. And that goes for his wife. If she's stupid enough to marry a split, it's her funeral. She wasn't dragged to the altar, so she knows the form. She heard 'em say in church she was taking him in sickness and in health, to have and to hold, and all the rest of it. She'll just have to share his little bit of bad luck, won't she?'

'But . . .'

'You want to understand something. Ever since the trial I've been laughing myself sick, thinking of me getting off and a split in trouble for planting that glove. Sometimes, I've been choking from laughter, ain't I, Flo?'

'Yes,' she said.

'It ain't often a bloke gets a chance to laugh as much as I have. Why don't you cheer up a bit and have a chuckle? It don't do to be sad. Doesn't the Bible tell us all to eat and drink for tomorrow we die?'

'Can't you understand . . .?'

'Or was it Dickens who wrote that?'

'How the hell should I know?' cried Craig desperately.

'There you go, destroying my faith in the splits. I've been brought up to think of 'em as smart, so much smarter than us simple villains. But you say you don't know who wrote that. It ain't right. What would your educated chief constable say about such simple ignorance?'

Craig turned and stepped towards the door.

'Are you going? Now that's a pity. I thought we'd have a nice little chat and you could tell me things, like how's my friend Mr. Miller what I haven't seen around for a while? They tell me he's got a nice wife and some lovely kids. I like kids. There just ain't nothing I wouldn't do for kids. I'm a real sucker for them.'

Craig reached the door, opened it, and went out. As the door clicked shut he heard Haggard begin to laugh once more.

Craig pressed the button to summon the lift. He had suffered the humiliation. Since when did men like Haggard feel compassion: since when did men like Haggard worry a fig about the terrible waves of tragedy that followed their crimes? Haggard didn't give a damn how McQueen was, so why should he suffer a second's worry over a man who was unjustly accused of lying, a wife who was tormented by her husband's misery, children persecuted by their fellow children, or the tragedy of a family about to be broken up? Suffer worry over such things? They were amusing.

 . . . . .

After Craig had been gone a while, Haggard felt restless and he paced the floor of the living-room. He wanted to be up and doing, but wasn't quite certain doing what. A booze-up with Grant? No, he didn't want to see Grant.

'What's eating you?' asked Florence.

He looked at her as she lay on the settee, house-coat falling away to reveal most of her legs. They were smart legs. She had a smart body. She was a smart brass, come to that, who knew most of the answers. Still, as smart as she was, he didn't want her right then.

'What's eating you?' she repeated.

'Belt up.'

'Why keep walking up and down the room?'

He crossed to the settee and brutally pulled her hair. He laughed as she tried to rake his hands with her nails. Now he knew what he wanted. Another woman. Looking down at her, he knew he wanted another woman. 'I'm going out.' He let go of her hair.

She rubbed her scalp. 'Where are we going?'

'You ain't going anywhere.'

'Why can't I go with you?' She sat up and angrily pulled her house-coat about her. 'You're going off to another woman,' she shouted.

'It's taken you long enough to find out.'

She called him all the obscene names she could think of. He slapped her face and she began to cry.

'What's wrong with me?' she asked desperately.

'You're all right when a bloke needs a drink because he's dying of thirst. But me, I want some champagne.'

'If you go I won't stay here. I swear I won't.'

'It's a free world for some.'

He went into the bedroom and changed into the grey charcoal striped suit which made him look so distinguished. When a bloke went up to The Smoke he needed to look distinguished.

She came into the room and sat on the bed. He looked at her. She was beautiful in an innocent kind of a way that made her really desirable. Some brasses became old before they were aged, but she could still look like someone fresh up from the country.

'What is it you want?' she demanded.

'Peace from your bloody nagging.'

'But she can't give you anything I can't.'

'She's dumb. We do everything by signs. It's peaceful.' He smiled and began to tell her what they did together.

She came off the bed in one smooth movement and flung

herself at him. She tried to claw his face. He hit her back on to the bed. He told her he'd send her a postcard and left.

She lay on the bed, face aching from the heavy blow. She despised herself for letting him treat her as he did, letting him gain pleasure from humiliating her, but could do nothing about it. People thought it was funny when a brass fell in love. In love? they'd sneer. For how much? But a brass could fall in love just like a duke's virginal horse-riding daughter. The trouble was, they usually fell for the one kind of man who needed them, the human degradation called a ponce. Haggard, like most villains, hated ponces, but the way he treated her was exactly the way a ponce would have treated her. She gave him not only her body, but also herself, something she had never before offered a man, and he scorned both.

She sat up and reached over to the bedside table for a cigarette. Since the 1958 Street Offences Bill upset the London trade, a local turf had become good ground for top-quality brass. So she could keep herself in luxury. Then why didn't she quit Haggard and go back on to her turf? She had saved money. She had a bank account. The bank manager knew her account stood in four figures, he also knew how much he had contributed. He was very nice. He advised her to invest the money and make the capital work, but she wanted it handy so that if she demanded a thousand quid they had to hand it over to her immediately.

Why didn't she leave Haggard? Why did she subject herself to humiliation after humiliation and allow her mind to be racked by jealousy?

What kind of woman was he after? Perhaps he went after colour. A lot of men did, because colour was different.

She pictured a tall Negress, with laughing face and big round lips, slim figure, and an erotic way of moving. He was coming up beside her, laying his hand on her ...

She cried out. She longed to kill herself and escape this torture, but knew she hadn't the courage. She loved him. He could kick her to death and she'd die loving him. She stubbed out the cigarette and went through to the living-room. Through the picture window she could look out over the roofs of Frindhurst to the sea. The sunlight was sparkling on the water, looking like an everlasting shower of sequins. She turned away and crossed to the cocktail cabinet. She poured herself out a very strong gin and French. He wouldn't be back at the earliest until after lunch the next day. She'd get as drunk as possible, as soon as possible. Drink dulled her jealousy.

14

WITH one day to go before Miller's appearance in the magistrates' court, Craig sat in the R.C.A. room trying for the third time to type out a witness report. Each time he began to type his mind remembered Dusty Miller and family and his hands ran amok.

The door opened and Detective Constable Nachton came in.

'Hullo, cock, actually busy? I thought you fellows in R.C.S. spent all the afternoons on the beach?'

'You thought wrong.'

'Hullo, hullo, life a bit of a grind?' Nachton was not the sort of a man to wonder whether Craig would rather have been left on his own. 'Has old man Barnard been getting on your wick? Treat him like you would a mother-in-law, that's my advice: keep out of his way as long as you can, and when you can't, just smile. Talking about mothers-in-law, how about a night out tonight with a couple of sheilas?'

'Not for me.'

'Now don't take fright so easily. I haven't grabbed the good-looking one and left you with the buck teeth. They've both got everything that's necessary and we won't be wasting our time.'

'I'm going round to Miller's tonight.'

Nachton looked vaguely surprised as he sat down on the edge of the desk. 'How is Dusty?'

'Not exactly bubbling over with joy.'

Inevitably, Nachton failed to realise any sarcasm had been intended. 'Isn't he? Bit of a thing for him tomorrow, I suppose. You can't say the evidence exactly favours him.'

'I don't know what the evidence is.'

'A bit solid. That's what I'd call it, a bit solid.'

'Has anyone really bothered to find out what the evidence is?'

'Barnard's been in charge of the investigations.'

'And you told me he wasn't worrying much.'

'I don't say he's rushed things, but he's been working. Don't forget the old saying that you can't make bricks without straw.'

'What's that supposed to mean?'

'Your pal Dusty is there in the deep end.'

Craig spoke bitterly. 'He didn't plant that glove.'

Nachton shrugged his shoulders. 'He's got my sympathy, but I'm not backing his side to win. Carpenter isn't changing his story for anyone.'

'Has anyone really investigated him?'

'They've done all the right things.'

'Is his business doing well?'

'He's not running another Marks and Sparks, but things are ticking over. Maybe he prefers it that way for the tax man.'

'What about his bank accounts?'

'As clean as a whistle and not a penny in 'em that shouldn't be.'

'When I went to his place and tried to buy a pair of Keelers' gardening gloves, the assistant told me they didn't stock 'em.'

'They stocked some for a while just before the robbery, but old man Carpenter reckoned they weren't good enough so he stopped having 'em.'

'Who's fool enough to believe that story?'

'There's no proof otherwise.'

'Were his stock figures checked?'

'Look, chum, the Frindhurst C.I.D. knows a little about its job. The gloves were in the shop before the robbery.'

'Could the entry in the books have been forged afterwards? What about the manufacturers? What do their records show?'

'Carpenter buys most of his stuff from people specialising in bankruptcy or salvaged stock. That crowd doesn't keep records.'

'Has the pressure been put on Carpenter?'

'No.'

'Why not?'

'Why ask me? I'm not the D.C.I. Anyway, what's the use of putting pressure on a bloke unless you know he's crooked? You just get a smack in the teeth from the bloke's M.P. Everybody writes to M.P.s these days. What's more, some of the M.P.s have even learned how to write back.'

Craig stared blankly at the typewriter and the third draft of the witness statement.

'Look, cock,' said Nachton, in an avuncular manner, 'it's rough to sit back and see one's mate clobbered, but sometimes that's the way of the world.'

Craig stood up and kicked his chair backwards. He went over to the side window and looked out and down at the bowling green on which two games were being played. 'And d'you continue to sit back and do nothing when you know the bloke's innocent?'

'How d'you know it?'

'Dusty says so.'

'D'you expect him to say anything else?'

Craig swung round. 'You know Dusty. He'd talk all night long, but that's all. When it came down to it, he wouldn't do anything to risk his pension. His pension meant far more than landing Haggard for the robbery.'

Nachton shrugged his very broad shoulders.

Craig suddenly felt desperately tired. If the ordinary policeman, sympathetic towards Miller, could not believe in his innocence, what chance was there that the magistrates or the judge and jury would? The jury were the public and the public, because of their subconscious rejection of the police, revelled in a chance to punish a policeman who had stepped, even fractionally, over the line.

Nachton moved off the desk. 'You won't come a-wenching, then?'

'No.'

'Too much celibacy makes a man mad. You know that, don't you?'

'I'm practically engaged to a girl in Repton,' muttered Craig.

'There's all the difference between being engaged and being practically engaged. One's dangerous whilst the other's as good as an invitation. Still, if you're willing to risk madness, you remain celibate. But never say I didn't warn you.' Nachton left the room.

Craig returned to his desk and sat down. He stared at the typewriter. What the hell was he doing, typing out an unimportant witness statement when Dusty was waiting to be thrown into the ring, like a bull at a bullfight, knowing that no matter how hard and well he fought he was doomed? Yet what else could he, Craig, do? He had tried to uncover the truth and had merely collected a very severe reprimand from the D.C.I. Fear of another reprimand wouldn't deter him if only there was something to deter him from—but where could he go, to try what?

.   .   .   .   .

The next morning Craig entered the magistrates' court through the witnesses' door and stood against the wall. He stared at Miller, in the dock, and then hastily looked away. Miller had looked as if he thought Craig had no right to be standing against a wall, free, whilst he was falsely charged with perjury.

The magistrates came into court. There were five: four men and one woman. Craig studied them. The chairman was old and crippled with arthritis, on his left was an over-sleek pudgy man who owned a shop, and at the end of the row was a hatchet-faced woman. If you distilled their minds and those of the other two men together, would you amass an ounce of understanding pity?

The case moved smoothly, delayed only by the need for the evidence to be taken in longhand for the depositions. Carpenter gave his evidence easily and concisely, Haggard was reasonably deferential, although clearly enjoying himself. Florence appeared to be overawed by the proceedings. When

Craig was called he struggled to tilt the evidence in favour of Miller, but was only too aware how unsuccessful he was.

The defence barely cross-examined the witnesses. At the conclusion the defence solicitor submitted there was no case to answer. There was a very short conference on the Bench and then it was held that there was a case to answer. Miller's solicitor reserved the defence and the case was put down for the next assize. A request for bail was being made when Miller began to shout.

'I didn't plant that glove.' He gestured with both hands. 'You've got to believe me, your Worships. I didn't plant it. They're lying, just as they did at the trial.'

'Be quiet,' ordered the chairman.

'I didn't do it.'

'You have received a very fair hearing.'

'D'you call it fair when you've sent me for trial when I didn't do anything? I'm innocent.'

'Do you wish me to find you in contempt of court?'

Miller turned until he could look at his wife who, despite all his pleas, had insisted on coming to the court. 'I didn't do it,' he shouted.

She sat at the end of a bench, an upright figure, her face drained of all emotion: her fingers constantly kneaded a small lace-edged handkerchief.

The uniformed constable by the side of the dock put his hand on Miller's shoulder. He whispered something. Miller slowly relaxed.

'There is no excuse for a scene of this nature,' said the chairman testily.

The request for bail was repeated. A uniformed superintendent said there was no objection. Bail was set at two sureties of a hundred pounds each.

Craig left the courtroom and walked along the corridor to the outside door. He stepped out into the sunshine. It seemed as if God Himself were laughing, to provide so lovely a day.

. . . . . .

Craig parked his car just beyond Carpenter's shop. He walked back to the shop. The assistant with the exploding hair style was gone, but his place was taken by a pimply youth whose greasy hair was almost as luxuriant.

'Is Carpenter in?' Craig demanded.

The youth, astonished by the harshness of his voice, stared at him.

'Is he in?'

'No, 'e ain't. 'E's in court.'

'The case finished over an hour ago.'

'Well I dunno, then.'

'You've no idea where he's gone?'

'I dunno.'

Craig left the shop and drove to the address Carpenter had given in court. The house was small, box-shaped, detached, in a row of precisely similar houses. The tiny garden in front was neglected. He knocked on the door and after a while Carpenter opened it.

Carpenter's beady eyes expressed first surprise and then a sly wariness. 'What d'you want?'

Craig pushed past him and stepped into the hall.

'You can't come in like that.'

'I'm in.'

'You ain't no right to do it.'

'I'm not worrying about rights.'

A drably dressed woman came through the far doorway into the hall and stared uncertainly at them. She asked if anything was wrong. Carpenter told her nothing was and to go back to the kitchen. After a moment's hesitation she did so.

Carpenter opened the door on his right and went into the room beyond. Craig followed him. It was a sitting-room, grossly overburdened with a large and shabby three-piece suite.

'Now, what is it?' asked Carpenter, with a feeble attempt to exert his authority.

'I want the truth.'

'I don't know what you mean.'

'How much were you paid for all those lies in court?'

'Here. You can't talk like that. I can have you for slander.'
'Go ahead and try.'
'You've no call to come here.'
'I'll keep coming until I get the truth.'
'The police have checked my story and ain't found nothing wrong with it.'
'That's why I'm still looking.'

Carpenter licked his lips with a tongue that flicked in and out. 'Look, life's difficult enough without you stirring up trouble. Suppose I was to pass over something?'

'Something?'
'You know.'
'Do I?'
'Gawd, you play it tight. Something like a hundred quid.'
'A bribe?'
'Nothing like that. There ain't no need for a bribe. You've got to understand, I was just——'

'You won't stop me with some dirty little bribe,' said Craig tightly.

'A hundred quid's a hundred quid. Suppose I was to stretch it a bit . . .'

'A thousand won't stop me. I'm going to nail you, you bastard.'

Carpenter's voice rose. 'What makes you so stupid? Why won't you take a hundred and fifty quid? What's it matter if he's been sent for trial? It ain't you. If he was so stupid as to go around shouting his mouth off he can't complain now if people believe what he said. Why's he so hot on putting anyone inside? It's not personal to him. Why don't he take his bung like any sensible——'

Craig hit Carpenter in the stomach. Carpenter doubled up, gasping, sounding as if his lungs had sprung a leak. He collapsed on to the floor.

Craig stared down at him. This was the first man he had ever hit, outside of self-defence. He found that his one real thought was a hope that Carpenter was in agony.

After a while Carpenter dragged himself up on to the nearest chair. When he saw Craig move, he flinched.

Craig walked past him and out of the room. The drab woman was standing by the kitchen door. She looked at him, but said nothing. He left the house and went up the weed-infested crazy-paving path to the low rusty wrought-iron gate.

.   .   .   .   .

That evening, at ten minutes to six, Craig was summoned by telephone to Barnard's office. Barnard sat behind his desk and Detective Inspector Everam stood to his right.

Barnard spoke in a tightly controlled, but angry, voice. 'We've received a second and more serious complaint from Carpenter. He claims you visited his house early this afternoon and threatened him in the most abusive manner. He further claims you struck him violently. Is this true?'

'No, sir.'

'Did you visit his house?'

'I did, sir.'

'Why?'

'To ask him a few questions.'

'Did you hit him?'

'No, sir.'

'He says you did.'

'Then he's lying. Has he seen a doctor for corroborative evidence?'

Barnard and Everam exchanged quick glances. 'His wife testified he has heavy bruising on his stomach,' said Barnard.

'Does she claim to have seen me hit her husband?'

'She was not in the room at the time.'

'Then her evidence doesn't amount to much, does it, sir? Perhaps Carpenter fell over something and injured himself that way.'

'You went to his house expressly against my orders.'

'It was in my own time, sir. I went as an individual and not as a police officer.'

'Don't be ridiculous.'

'I had signed off duty, sir.'

'You know damn well that's nonsense. Carpenter believed you to be on duty.'

'I can hardly be held responsible for his beliefs.'

'You hit him. You went there, questioned him, lost your temper and hit him because you've been fool enough to get emotionally involved in the case.'

'I did not hit him, sir.'

'Then why should he claim you did?'

'To try to discredit me.'

'Discredit you?'

'He tried to bribe me to stop questioning him about the glove he says he sold. He offered me a hundred pounds and then a hundred and fifty. He called me a fool for not taking the money. By offering me a bribe he was really admitting he was lying about the glove. Since the bribe failed, he's trying to discredit my evidence before I give it.'

Barnard pushed back his chair and stood, put his hands in his pockets, and paced up and down. 'I believe you hit him,' he said angrily. He came to a stop. 'You've forgotten everything you've ever been taught about the duties of a policeman. Like Miller, you've begun to think you are the law. Carpenter will be seen and a statement will be taken from him. If the evidence warrants it, you'll suffer the appropriate consequences.'

'Yes, sir.'

'Whatever happens, I shall make out a D report, dealing with your deliberate disobedience of my orders and this will be sent to the assistant chief constable, R.C.S. Do you understand?'

'Yes, sir.'

Barnard pulled his hands free of his pockets, went back to his chair, and sat down. When next he spoke his voice was expressing only a sad exasperation. 'Damn it, man, why couldn't you leave things to the people best equipped to deal with them?'

'Because I don't think they were trying to deal with them.'

There was a short silence. Barnard's furious voice broke it. 'Get out,' he shouted.

Craig turned and walked out of the room.

Everam waited until the door shut. 'I'm afraid he's——' he began.

'Get out,' shouted Barnard for the second time. He watched his D.I. leave. Goddam the chief constable, he thought wildly. Those who believed Barnard to be a man without emotions would have been surprised to see the look of anguish on his face.

15

CRAIG visited Miller's house that night and was sitting in the small dining-room with them when they heard the telephone ring. A moment later there was a knock on the door and the landlady looked in to say the call was for them. Miller started to get up, but his wife said she'd take it and left the room.

Miller stubbed out one cigarette and lit another. He had become a compulsive chain smoker: his fingers were badly stained and he had developed an almost constant cough.

Craig, looking across at Miller, found himself wondering why the other wasn't showing more fight. Dusty seemed mentally to have collapsed, so that now he was only capable of sitting hunched up, deep in his own misery. Craig suddenly cursed himself for thinking as he had just done. When a man knew himself to be innocent of a criminal charge but was faced with overwhelming and apparently incontrovertible evidence pointing to his guilt, how could he think in terms of fighting?

Violet Miller returned to the room and Craig saw, with a sense of shock, the tears in her eyes. 'What's happened?' he asked harshly.

She looked at him, but said nothing.

Craig's words had drawn Miller's attention to his wife. 'What's the matter, love?'

'It was filthy,' she muttered. 'It was a man, laughing, telling me you were going to go to prison for years and years. He said prison was the proper place for policemen. He said he hoped they'd put you inside for ten years and how would the kids like a jail-bird as a father?'

Miller stubbed out the cigarette he had been smoking with such force that the paper split and the tobacco spilt out. 'What kind of voice? Did he talk about prison or the nick?'

'He called it the nick and said cozzpots and splits, but I knew what he meant. Albert, Albert, they're not going to put you in jail, are they? They couldn't. Please, they couldn't.'

'It was Haggard,' whispered Miller.

'I think he was drunk.'

Craig left the house just as soon as he could. He was too much of a coward willingly to stay amongst such misery.

.   .   .   .   .

At 9 a.m. the following morning, a Thursday, Craig reported to the central police station and signed the attendance register, looked through the mail and read the two Telex messages, then left. He drove to Telton and parked his car in the forecourt of the luxury flats. Two cars away was the cream coloured Buick.

He left the worn-out police car and went up to the Buick Riviera. It was a large, handsome car, with the novel feature—for England—of retractable lights which were masked by shields, similar in design to the frontal grill, when not in use. Haggard almost certainly had bought the car second-hand, yet even so it represented something he, Craig, could never hope to own. These days, crime did pay—for the clever professional.

A voice spoke from just behind him. 'Trying to nick me for an out-of-date licence?'

Craig turned and faced Haggard. Haggard was wearing dark flannel trousers, a nylon shirt, a fitted sports jacket, and a patterned silk scarf about his neck. He looked immaculate.

'I'll nick you,' said Craig.

'For a licence?'

'For anything I can.'

Haggard became more wary as he took the measure of this split's hatred. 'Are you threatening me?'

'The moment I can land you, I will, without bothering about threats.'

'You've got a long, long wait, sonny boy.'

'I'm in no hurry.'

'You were last time I saw you.'

'Today's another day. Sooner or later you'll have to pull another job and that's when I'll get you.'

'I've made enough to retire on, sonny. I won't be doing another job all the time your pal Miller's in the nick.'

'There won't be much left out of your last job. It'll have cost you a fortune to fake the evidence and buy that witness: the mouthpiece'll have shaken you down for every penny he could. You'll be looking around for another job. I'll be waiting for you when you pull it.'

'The sergeant's kids'll be waiting, too, won't they? But they'll be waiting for years and years. He'll be doing bird until his wife's hair's gone grey.'

'Maybe.'

Haggard was infuriated by Craig's calmness. He pushed past Craig, deliberately bumping into him, and unlocked the driving door of the car.

'Going out for long?' asked Craig.

'What's it to you?'

'I'll be tailing you. I wondered whether we'll be gone for long?'

'You ain't tailing me nowhere.'

'I'll be trying.'

'You ain't got nothing on me.'

'I've a lot and the next task is to make it stick.'

Haggard climbed into the car and slammed the door shut. He switched on the engine and it fired immediately. He backed out, swung round, accelerated fiercely forward and immediately had to brake harshly as a woman, wheeling a pram, stepped across the exit to the forecourt. He sounded the horn and as soon as the way was clear drove out on to the road, immediately in front of a heavily laden lorry.

Craig watched the Buick until it was out of sight. He had ruffled Haggard's feelings, which was something: but it was a very small, insignificant, and childish something. Haggard was on the winning side and knew it. He'd carried out a robbery, been tried, and found not guilty so that he could never be charged with it again. In addition, he'd made certain a detective-sergeant was charged with perjury. What villain could ask for more?

Craig returned to his car and leaned against the bonnet. He didn't know why he'd come here. There'd been no definite plan in his mind at the beginning and there was none now. He looked at his watch. A quarter past ten. He should be over at Evely, working with the local police on a breaking and entering. If his absence was noted and reported he'd finally be for the high jump.

He looked up at the tall, ugly concrete and glass building. Was Florence, the red-headed whore, up there? She had given Haggard an alibi and although she was lying no one could prove she was. She and Haggard had been together a long time now, considering who they were: men like Haggard usually changed their women nearly as often as their socks.

Craig walked up to the main doors of the building. She would know a lot about Haggard's operations. She might know how much Carpenter was paid and who actually paid him.

Craig crossed the hall to the lift and went up to the fifth floor. He knocked on the door of flat 5A. After some twenty seconds Florence opened the door.

She was wearing a lace-edged blouse, a fashionable short skirt, stockings, and a pair of crocodile leather shoes. Her auburn hair was short, discreetly waved, and carefully brushed. She looked virginal.

She spoke with bitter anger. 'He ain't in.'

He was certain her anger did not all stem from finding him on the doorstep. He wondered whether she and Haggard had just had a row. 'I know he's out.'

'Then you also know there ain't nothing for you here.' She went to slam the door shut.

Craig placed his foot between door and jamb and his mind flicked back to the time when Dusty had done that, on the day

137

he found the glove in the pocket of Haggard's trousers. Craig put his shoulder to the door and pushed and she had to step quickly backwards to maintain her balance. He entered the hall.

'You've no right to do that,' she said shrilly.

'There aren't many rights left in the case.'

'What d'you want?'

'Just to ask you a question or two.'

'I ain't talking until he gets back.'

'I can't wait that long. He won't be back for hours.'

'How d'you know?'

He studied her. She was fidgeting with her skirt as if unable to keep her fingers still. If she had had a row with Haggard, it had probably been over another woman. When a brass, who led a very lonely life, fell for a man, she fell for him hook, line, and sinker no matter how he treated her. Was Haggard treating her with open contempt because she had fallen for him?

'How d'you know he'll be gone a long time?' she repeated shrilly.

'I've been watching him.'

'So what's he doing?'

'He went off with a woman. You can fill in the rest better than I can.'

'You lying split,' she shouted.

He shrugged his shoulders.

She stopped fiddling with her skirt. She raised her right hand and brushed a hair away from her forehead. 'Why've you been tailing him?'

'I surely don't have to explain that one to you?'

She turned round, suddenly, and went into the living-room. He followed her.

She came to a halt by the settee. 'He hasn't got another woman,' she said.

'What's the matter—jealous?'

'He wouldn't go after another woman.'

'You don't sound very certain.'

She walked over to the cocktail cabinet and poured herself

out a whisky which she drank neat. 'Well?' she asked, as she turned round.

'Well what?'

'What the hell d'you want here?'

'First things coming first, I'll take a drink.'

She hesitated for a while, then reached down and brought out another glass from the lower shelf in the cabinet. She poured out two whiskies and handed him the second glass.

He went over to the settee. She crossed to the nearer leather arm-chair and sat down. 'Since when have you been tailing him?' she asked.

'Since a few days ago. Didn't he tell you about it? He spotted me, but just didn't seem to care what was happening.'

'How d'you mean, care?'

'Didn't care me seeing who he's spending all his time with.'

'He's not spending all his time with anyone.'

Craig drank.

'All right,' she said loudly, 'so he's been with someone in The Smoke.'

'Not in London.'

'I tell you, he's been in London.'

'Not recently.'

'But he said——' She cut short her words. 'Where's he been then?'

'Nowhere.'

'You've just said——'

'Nowhere outside Telton. The two of them must be too busy to travel much.'

'You're lying,' she shouted.

He smiled.

She finished her drink, stood up, and crossed to the cocktail cabinet where she poured herself out her third whisky. She drank half of it before she returned to the chair. She lit a cigarette. 'Where do they go in Telton?'

'Her place isn't far from here.'

'How often?'

'If you mean how often does he go to her house, practically every time he leaves here.'

She scraped off into an ash-tray the barely formed ash on her cigarette. 'Who is she?'

Craig leaned over and picked up one of the copies of the *Saturday Evening Post* that were neatly stacked under the table by the side of his chair. He opened it.

'Who is she?' demanded Florence for the second time, her voice once more shrill.

Craig replied without looking up. 'A local. Like I told you, her place isn't far away.' He turned over several pages of the magazine.

'Is he with her now?'

'Yes.'

'You came here just after he left. You couldn't know what he'd been doing: there wasn't time.'

'He picked her up in the forecourt. She was waiting by his car.'

'He . . . he wouldn't do that.'

'Are you thinking about the old saying of never using your own doorstep?' He dropped the magazine on to his lap and studied her. 'What's got him wandering so hard? Have you been laid off for a day or two?'

'You dirty split.'

'It happens, even to the nicest lady.'

'What's she like?'

'Who?'

'You know who I mean. What's she like?'

'The woman he's with now? Quite something. The kind that makes a man eat a plateful of oysters first.'

'Is she a spade?'

He closed the magazine and replaced it under the table before he answered her. 'It's odd you should ask that. There's a sight more than a touch of the tar-brush in the lady.'

In a wild surge of fury she threw her glass on to the floor. The pile of the carpet was so thick that the glass did not break.

'I suppose it's a case of variety being the spice of life?' he suggested.

She began to swear.

He finished his drink and was about to speak, to put the first of several questions to her, when she dropped her cigarette into the ash-tray. She ran across to the door.

'Are you coming?' she shouted, as she came to a halt in the doorway.

His throat suddenly felt thick. 'Coming?'

She went out. Seconds later, he heard a door crash against a wall and she called out again.

He put his glass down on the small table. Vaguely he was aware of the certainty that to continue was to be a fool. But that knowledge was forced to the back of his mind as he visualised her as she might be now. His throat was so dry that he had difficulty in swallowing: there was a pounding in his ears.

He stood up, looked round the room, and walked out of the living-room into the hall. It was crazy, but he found the furnishings of the hall of the utmost interest. He could have stood there and studied them for hours.

She appeared in the open doorway of the bedroom. Her face had altered completely because of its expression of malevolent ecstasy. Behind her was the bedroom in which Dusty had found the glove. He had to know how that room was furnished. He pushed past her and went in.

In the centre was an oval bed, eight feet across at its widest point. The cover depicted a tapestry-like hunting scene: if she slept on the right-hand side, the fox was exactly where her belly would be. The carpet was a light grey, with a pile even thicker than the one in the living-room: the curtains were a crimson velvet. Contrasting wallpapers were on the walls and ceiling. The dressing-table looked to be a valuable antique: a set of heavy silver toilet articles was on the top of it.

She came up to him and pressed against him so that he could feel some of her curves. She was murmuring a few words over and over again and they sounded almost as if she were moaning.

She began to caress him, in a way that he had never before

experienced. Vaguely, he thought that he'd never before known a woman could caress like this. They said that a man only learned when it was too late, but that a woman was born with the knowledge. God knows where her knowledge ended.

She moved her body against his so that he was reminded of a snake. A venomous green mamba. She gripped his right hand and pulled it down on herself. She pressed so hard against his hand that he was afraid of hurting her, but she seemed oblivious of pain.

He undressed her, exactly according to her commands. It took a long time. Later, when his mind insisted on remembering all they had done together while he undressed her, he was to suffer utter shameful disbelief.

Once naked, she lay down on the bed. He struggled to take off his own clothes, but as soon as he had pulled off his jacket and dropped it on to the floor she stopped his going further and ordered him to one of the built-in cupboards. She told him to wear one of the jackets that was hanging there. As if in a dream, he took a brown and yellow flecked Harris tweed sports coat off its hanger and put it on. She called him over to the bed. As she kissed him with a frightening, hysterical passion, she caressed the coat he was wearing with frenzied force.

When he could wait no longer he ripped his clothes from himself.

. . . . .

Craig lay on the oval bed and looked down at his own body and for once it seemed to be a shameful thing. He hurriedly dressed.

The door of the bedroom opened and Florence came in. She was dressed and once more looking virginal, every line of malevolent passion gone from her face.

He took a packet of cigarettes from his pocket. He tried to speak casually. 'You must have been around when Carpenter came here?'

She spat, and her spittle landed high up on his right cheek. It rolled down and on to his coat. 'Get out.'

'But you——'

'D'you think I'd grass on him? To a split? Get out.' Her voice rose still higher. 'Get out. Get out.'

He walked out of the bedroom. He reached the front door of the flat, opened it, and went out on to the landing. Before he could close the door it was slammed shut behind him.

Bewildered, he looked at his watch. It was just eleven o'clock. He listened to the watch to see if it was still going because he was so certain that hours had passed since he had checked on the time down in the forecourt.

He pressed the button to summon the lift. Somewhere in his mind he seemed to be crying.

. . . .

Craig returned to his digs at seven-thirty that night. There was a letter from Daphne in the hall. He put it in his pocket, unopened, and went into the dining-room where the sour-faced old termagant of a landlady served him with boiled mutton that was both tough and tasteless.

As soon as he had finished his meal he went up to his bedroom, the only room where he could be certain the landlady wouldn't suddenly appear to check on what he was doing.

He sat down on the uncomfortable, squeaking bed and took Daphne's letter from his pocket. After a long hesitation he opened and read it. It was written in her usual lively and affectionate style and she ended up by saying that if he still thought she was going to wait to marry him until he had completed his sergeant's course he'd better see a head-shrinker. He put the letter back in its envelope.

He was so tired that he decided to go to bed and he began to undress. He hung up his trousers and coat in the battered wardrobe and began to unbutton his shirt. There was a loose thread on the second button and he looked down. Wrapped once round the button was a single thread of a rough brown and yellow speckled wool which he immediately identified as having come from the coat Florence had made him wear. He pulled the thread free and was about to throw it away when he stopped himself. A few seconds later he took a matchbox from his pocket, emptied out the matches, and put the thread into it.

16

MILLER's trial was held on the 21st July. The courtroom was filled with spectators and a further hundred of the public had to be refused admission. The disgrace of a detective who had believed that justice consisted in the punishment of the guilty was a great attraction.

The newspapers gave the trial great prominence. A leader in a right-wing paper said that Miller's trial demonstrated to the world that British justice was quite incorruptible and a well-known writer wrote in a left-wing paper that Miller's trial demonstrated to the world that British justice was utterly corrupted.

Only his family remembered who McQueen was or thought about him. He had been sent home from the hospital because the doctors could do nothing for him and his continued presence at the hospital was a bad advertisement for their own skills. Mrs. McQueen had been advised to put in a claim on behalf of her husband for compensation as the victim of a crime involving bodily harm. One day there would be a small monetary payment.

The trial proceeded smoothly. Haggard, Florence Jones, and Carpenter made good witnesses. Haggard freely admitted to his past criminal history and said that it was because he had always willingly paid the debt he owed to society that this attempt by a detective-sergeant to make him pay a debt he had not contracted enraged him so. The jury were impressed by his words. Juries are often impressed, but seldom impressive.

Miller's greatest handicap as a witness was that he was telling the truth. When he admitted he had searched Haggard's flat without the authority of a search warrant the jury immediately assumed that because he had sinned in the minor matter, he had sinned also in the major one. Juries are ruled by logic, but are seldom logical.

Miller was found guilty of the abominable crime of perjury. From the way he acted when the verdict was delivered, he had been naive enough to believe the verdict could have been otherwise. However, the warders by his side soon shut him up.

The judge was a very righteous man. 'A policeman is in a position of trust,' he said, in his rich, fruity, mellow voice, 'a trust placed in him by the general public, a trust rightly held by most to be sacred. Because of this trust the British policemen are almost the only ones in the world to go about their duties unarmed. That is a glorious thing. You, Miller, have betrayed that trust; you have imperilled the unique character of the British police.'

'I'm innocent,' shouted Miller.

'Do not interrupt me,' said the judge, angrily dismissing an irrelevance. 'When a man goes out of his way to betray his country, knowing full well what he is doing, he must be prepared to suffer the consequences. I sentence you to seven years' imprisonment.'

Miller swayed slightly.

The judge left the court through the door at the back of the dais. Miller was led down the stairs at the back of the dock.

Craig walked slowly out of the courtroom. Seven years which, with remission for good conduct, could be reduced to four years and eight months. Four years and eight months during which Miller would be subjected to vicious persecution at the hands of all other prisoners because nothing gave them greater pleasure than to persecute a split caught up in the same hell as themselves. Four years and eight months during which Violet Miller would have to struggle with every last ounce of strength to try to keep herself and her children fed, housed, and clothed.

. . . . .

The summer continued. A Test match was lost by an umpire's disputed decision, the government yet again declared itself the guardian of the people's liberty at the same time as it whittled away a little more of that liberty, and a local council in Lancashire threw a tenant out of a council house because he kept two cats where regulations only allowed one.

On Saturday night, September the 14th, after a day of rain which at times had been of almost tropical intensity, three tearaways began their first full-scale job.

They had graduated by way of juvenile delinquency. No one had taught them that crime did not pay, all the evidence was to the contrary, so they naturally tried for the big league. They decided to do the warehouse in the trading estate on the north side of Gresham which housed electrical goods, especially things like transistor radios and portable TV sets which were so easily disposed of to the fences. Being tearaways and not yet even small-time villains they hardly planned the robbery, but spent all that day working out how they'd spend the money they'd make.

At 11.53 p.m. they stole a large van and drove to the trading estate and along the outer road to the warehouse.

The leader forced the side door with a jemmy. The noise was considerable, but as the trading estate was deserted throughout the week-end they had only to worry about police patrol cars.

The leader went along the narrow, dingy passage and into the main storage area. He crossed to the main doors, unbolted them, and swung them open. The van drove in. The other two climbed out of the cab of the van and looked around at the cartons and cases neatly stacked in separate bays, all filled with small electrical goods. It was so dead easy. A blind man could have done it. Like people said, firms these days begged to be done.

Just before the leader gave the order to start loading, he looked up and at the end of the warehouse. Here, a short staircase led up to a small block of offices and a light was just visible now that the van's headlights were turned off. The leader flashed his torch at the offices and to his surprise an elderly man came into view. For a moment the youths, shocked to discover the warehouse had been guarded, stared up at the night watchman, and he, shocked to discover that the noises which had awoken him were caused by this breaking and entering, stared down at them.

The watchman moved first, to hurry back to the room he had just left to telephone the police. The tearaways came back to life. Shouting wildly, the leader raced towards the stairs.

The watchman was an old age pensioner who made an extra six pounds a week by sleeping at the warehouse rather than at home. Age had crippled him and when he tried to run his legs seemed to have lost the ability to obey his brain so that he could do nothing but shuffle. He had only just reached the table in the room and put his hand on the telephone receiver when the first tearaway appeared in the doorway. Fear flooded his mind and he did not even try to lift the receiver off its cradle. He stood there, quite still, right up to the moment the wooden pick-axe handle came smashing down on his head. He collapsed to the ground, semi-conscious, the world a muffled place of horror and galloping pain. A piece of rag was stuffed into his mouth and for a few frantic seconds it choked him, then he managed to breathe. His hands were wrenched round behind his back and tied tightly together.

He heard them rip the telephone cable out of its socket. This was followed by the noise of their feet clattering down the uncovered wooden stairs. The darkness of unconsciousness hovered across his mind, but never closed in to give him relief from the blinding pain in his head.

After what seemed hours he heard a sound that bewildered him until he identified it as the noise of a vehicle's engine. The thugs were clearing out with whatever they had stolen. He groaned, but the gag throttled the sound.

More time passed. As everything remained quiet he could be certain they had gone. He began to struggle with the bonds. Eventually he freed his hands and tore the gag out of his mouth. There was another telephone in one of the back rooms and he staggered through to find it in working order. He lifted the receiver and dialled 999. After he had reported the robbery, he collapsed to the floor.

. . . . .

Craig was awakened by the ringing of the telephone. He switched on the bedside light and looked at his wrist watch. It was four-twenty-five in the morning. At such a time the call must be for him. He hoped his landlady would not have been made too furious by the call.

He went downstairs to the telephone. The station sergeant told him there'd been a breaking and entering in a warehouse on the north trading estate at Gresham, the night watchman had received serious head injuries, and he was to report there immediately.

He returned to his room, dressed, then left the house and walked the quarter of a mile to the central police station. He climbed into the R.C.S. Humber and persuaded the engine to fire at the fourth attempt.

He reached Gresham and saw a patrolling constable who directed him to the trading estate. Once there, he soon found the warehouse and he parked the car behind two police Austins and went inside.

Overhead fluorescent lights had been switched on and the whole of the interior was brilliantly lit. In the centre of the open floor space four men stood round a small patch of dirty grease in which a tyre had left a pattern of its tread. One of the men was trying to photograph the mark and was swearing as light was constantly being reflected up from portable searchlights to dazzle the camera lens.

Craig was called across to the D.I. who gave him his orders. 'I want you to work with the others until you've got the picture. The intruders forced open the side door down there, came through and opened the main doors for a lorry to drive in. The night watchman says there weren't any preliminary sounds to make him suspicious, but he's obviously lying and was fast asleep. He came on to that balcony up there, saw three men down here, and tried to get to the telephone. One of the thugs reached him first and half smashed his skull in.'

'Did he see their faces, sir?'

'He says the bloke who hit him didn't have anything over his face, but from his description it could have been anyone from Frankenstein to Mussolini.'

Craig, after a few more words, left the D.I. and went across to help a detective constable and two uniformed constables to carry out a visual search of the warehouse. He slowly worked along the south wall, moving in and out of the bays. Everywhere were cartons and boxes that had been ripped open to see what were their contents and then left. He came across case after case containing coffee percolators, toasters, irons, and kettles, but not one with food mixers, wireless or TV sets. On two occasions the top row of goods in a case had obviously been handled and he took the things over to the pile, by the far doors, which was waiting the attention of the finger-print expert.

Craig, as he continued to work, mentally checked the facts of the case as he now knew them. The watchman had seen his assailant, but his description was useless. Would he be able to give a better description when he recovered from the shock of his attack? It was unlikely. An eye-witness description was always suspect, no matter how honestly given, because an eye-witness seldom saw what he thought he did. When an old man, terrified, desperately trying to summon help, was faced by someone about to knock him out, the odds against his giving an accurate description were very considerable. In any case, he had only seen one of them close to.

Craig stood still and shone his torch against a wall of wooden packing cases which had not been disturbed. Accept the fact that the watchman would never be able to give a good description; accept the risk that the men responsible for this robbery might be caught almost immediately through their own stupidity when it came to flogging the stolen goods; accept the fact that a hundred and one things could go wrong, but also that they could go right; accept his own actions precisely for what they were, admitting no self-delusory excuses or explanations. . . .

He turned round. The other searchers were on the far side of the shed, the D.I. had gone up with three men to the offices, and the finger-print detective sergeant had begun the mammoth task of testing for prints all the goods in the large pile on the floor. Craig walked along the shed to the side door which had been forced. The crowbar they'd used had splintered the wood of the door and jamb directly and also indirectly, at the point where the lock had torn away. Jagged pieces of wood stuck out in every direction. The whole area had been photographed, but because artificial light was a very poor substitute for daylight in this sort of work, a much closer investigation of the woodwork and more detailed photographs would be taken during the morning, especially to see if the crowbar had left any distinctive pattern in the wood.

Craig took a matchbox from his pocket and emptied out of it the short strand of wool, brown with yellow speckles. He wedged the strand behind one of the very jagged pieces of wood broken free by the lock. He replaced the matchbox in his pocket and went back to his previous task.

. . . . .

The damaged door and jamb of the warehouse were examined again just after eight o'clock in the morning. A clearer picture was taken of the crowbar mark at the top of the door.

The D.I., bleary-eyed and yawning, waited until the photographer was satisfied he had finished and then pushed past the photographer and made a close visual inspection of the door from top to bottom. Half-way down, caught behind a jagged splinter of wood, he saw a strand of wool, brown with yellow speckles. He demanded to know why this hadn't been found before. No one pointed out that this was the first examination in broad daylight. The D.I. was dog-tired, which meant he was not a man you explained anything to.

After photographs had been taken, the D.I. dropped the strand of wool into a small test-tube. He wedged the wool in position with plastic foam, corked the tube, initialled the label and wrote out time and date of discovery. He handed the tube to a constable to take to his car. The D.I. moved round to examine the door and jamb from all angles. When the cye was level with the jagged piece of wood, it was clear it stuck out into the doorway space. It must have caught one of the men's coats—the height showed it would be a coat—and pulled this length of wool out of it. This was the first piece of luck they had had.

. . . . .

The two detectives parked the car in the hospital car-park and entered by the main entrance. The porter directed them up to the male surgical ward. There, a belligerent ward sister tried to bar their way but reluctantly stepped aside when they explained the reason for their visit.

They went over to the end bed, ringed by curtains. Klinton, head heavily bandaged, stared up at them as they came through the gap in the curtains.

'Local C.I.D.,' said the elder of the two, and he introduced them both. 'How's it going?'

'Dreadful,' muttered Klinton.

'Got a headache?'

' 'Eadache? Gawd, it's splitting.' He looked, because of the bandage and the colour of his skin, older and sicker than he was.

'Haven't they given you anything for it?'

'Nothing they give me don't do no good. I've been near killed, that's what I've been.'

'We've come along to see whether now you're fully conscious you can help us a bit more?'

'I don't remember nothing but lookin' down and seein' 'em with their torches and one of 'em coming for me with the 'andle and belting me. I can tell you, I thought me last 'our 'ad come. They're all the same today. I fought in the first war, but look what they did to me.'

'How about the bloke who smashed you up? You must have had quite a good look at his face?'

'It's all so I can't remember nothing about it now.'
'I'm sure you can tell us something. Was this man's face a square or a round one?'
'I tell you, I don't remember nothing.'
The detectives continued to question Klinton, but every answer was the same. In the end the elder man asked whether Klinton would recognise the intruder should the two of them ever come face to face again.
'It's all so 'azy. I'm an old man and I fought in the first war and this is what they done for me. It ain't right.'

. . . . . .

On Tuesday the D.I. at Gresham had a visit from the county detective superintendent.
'Getting anywhere?' asked the detective superintendent, as he stepped into the D.I.'s room.
'We're moving, sir.'
'In which direction? Give it to me on the line, Joe. Are you getting anywhere?'
'We've that thread that was torn out of one of their coats.'
'There's just one thing, isn't there? You need the coat to go with it.'
'Quite, sir.'
'Look, I want to know if you've got anywhere towards smoking out the men who did the job?'
'Not yet, sir. Unfortunately, the night watchman is almost senile and swears he can't remember anything. He's not even certain that the man who hit him had two arms and two legs.'
'All right, so that lead's dead. Have you put out a general call on all merchants of violence?'
'I'm just about to.'
'Don't wait until winter's with us. The bloke may have bought himself a new suit by then.'
'Yes, sir,' said the D.I. stiffly.
'Get R.C.S. on to it. This is supposed to be their line of country.'
'Very well, sir.'

'Now look, Joe, I want results, and fast. I've the assistant chief constable on my back, so I'm jumping on your back and staying there until something breaks.'

. . . . .

Craig knocked on the door of Chief Inspector Barnard's office in the middle of the afternoon. He went in. Barnard, working in shirtsleeves, looked up. 'Yes?'

'Was the warehouse job in Gresham reported to you at all, sir? The one where the night watchman was severely coshed.'

'There's been no report through to me. It's a county matter.'

'Yes, sir. I've just had a request through from the county force to investigate all known villains of violence to see if any of them own a Harris tweed coat which matches the thread found caught in the door of the warehouse.'

Barnard put down his pencil. 'Can't you get on with a job like that without referring to me? I've too much on my plate without worrying about every job R.C.S. does.'

'I'm sorry, sir, but Haggard is on the list.'

Barnard leaned back in his chair. 'Well?'

'If it should be him, sir, and he's got the coat, I think I ought to have someone with me when I find the coat.'

Barnard rested his elbows on the arms of the chair. 'What are you getting at? That he might accuse you of planting the coat?'

'It's a risk I'd rather not take, sir.'

'Oh, well, I suppose so. Nachton can go with you and I'll square Telton on his behalf.' He yawned. 'Was it much of a job?'

'About a thousand quid's worth of electrical apparatus, sir.'

'O.K. Carry on and let me know the result.'

Craig left and searched the station for Detective Constable Nachton. He found him in the canteen, drinking tea and playfully trying to date the middle-aged woman who worked in the kitchen and who received the proposals with embarrassing coyness.

The two detectives drove to Telton and parked in the forecourt of the flats. Nachton, who had been relating the course of his latest seduction, expressed his annoyance at Craig's total lack of interest as he climbed out of the car. Once standing on the forecourt, he accused Craig of being something less than a man. To his annoyance, Craig ignored the insult.

They took the lift up to the fifth floor. Craig knocked on the door of flat 5A. Haggard opened the door.

'Well, well,' said Haggard. 'I'm real popular. No B.O.'

'Can we have a word with you?'

'Always ready to have a word with the C.I.D. Co-operation with the forces of law and order.' Haggard's sense of humour —engendered by his knowledge that there wasn't a split in the country could touch him—was elephantine. 'Welcome to my humble home.'

Haggard led them through to the living-room. Florence was on the settee, feet tucked under her, reading a magazine and eating chocolates. When she saw Craig her face went white. Craig did not look at her after the first quick glance.

'Have a fag?' said Haggard, and picked up a heavy silver cigarette case. 'It was presented to me by some of my friends. You know, like they do to the manager of I.C.I.'

Nachton, about to comment on the impossibility of Haggard's having any friends, for once exercised some discretion and checked his words as he noticed the expression on Craig's face. He assumed, with an ironic error, that Craig was suffering mentally because it was in this flat that his mate, Dusty Miller, had bought his own disgrace.

Craig took a cigarette from the silver cigarette box. Haggard flicked open a gold lighter. 'Not a bad little lighter.'

'Not bad.'

'There ain't nothing like gold, is there?'

'No, nothing.'

'Pity they don't give you blokes a chance to enjoy using it. It's a scandal the way they keep you blokes skint, ain't it?'

Florence stood up, but Haggard immediately asked her to sit down and help entertain their honoured guests. She hesitated, then sat down.

'What about poor Mr. Miller?' Haggard tried not to smile.

'What about him?' answered Craig.

'How is he?'

'Not too bad.'

'I don't suppose the police give Mrs. Miller any sort of a pension?'

'No, they don't.'

'That's real rough: I mean it, it's real rough. Now I bet she's nice: genuine nice. Is she?'

'Why should you worry?'

'Me? Mate, I'm not insensitive. If she's nice, I want to know, so as I can feel sorry for her. I want to understand how difficult it'll be for her to bring up her two kids without any real money coming in.'

'Very difficult indeed.'

'I suppose she can always go to the Assistance people. They're nice and generous, always provided you're very polite and smile at their little jokes. D'you think she'll know enough to be very polite to them?'

'I expect so.'

Haggard was tired of baiting a detective who seemed to have developed an unending ability to absorb insults. He lit a cigarette. 'All right, chum, what d'you want?'

'To hear where you were last Saturday night.'

'Last Saturday?' Haggard smiled. 'What's the problem?'

'A job was done.'

'You don't tell me.'

'A thousand quid's worth of electrical equipment was stolen from a warehouse.'

Haggard spoke angrily. 'A thousand, and you come bothering me? Didn't anyone tell you I left kindergarten a bloody long time ago?' He spoke to Florence. 'A job worth a mere thousand and he comes bothering me. Ain't that a laugh?'

She did not smile.

'Where were you last Saturday night?' repeated Craig.

Haggard swung round. 'You get me straight. You ain't persecuting me for every twopenny-halfpenny job just because your mate went crook. It don't matter to you where I was last Saturday.'

'Then you're refusing to answer?'

'What if I am?'

'It's significant.'

'It don't signify nothing. I was here, that's where I was, in me own flat. So put that down in your little black notebook and stuff it.'

'Is there anyone who can support your alibi?'

'It don't need supporting.'

'Then you were on your own?'

'Flo was with me.'

'Nobody else? No one whose word would carry more conviction—if that's not a painful expression for you?'

'Look, mate, you don't bleeding well come here insulting me. I wouldn't do a piddling job like that, not if you was to pay me.'

'Why? You're getting old. Maybe you're no good for the big jobs any more.'

'If I do a job it'll be big and you'll know all about it. A thousand quid? You splits don't know enough to tell the time. A thousand . . .'

'May we have a look at your clothes?'

Haggard's voice hardened and lost much of its bluster. 'Why?'

'In connection with enquiries we're making about this job last Saturday.'

'You ain't looking at nothing of mine.'

'Scared?'

'I ain't never been scared of a split.'

'You sound scared of what we'll find.'

'There ain't nothing to find because I weren't out last Saturday.'

'Then why be so afraid of us looking at your clothes?'

Haggard stubbed out the cigarette he had been smoking and lit another. 'Suppose I tell you you ain't got no warrant so you can go jump?'

'I'll get a warrant.' Craig spoke jeeringly. 'You're dead scared, Haggard. You did that job last Saturday and now everyone's going to find out how small-time you've become.

Three of you doing a job and all you could get out of it was a thousand. Tearaways straight out of Borstal could better that.'

'Go and bloody look at me clothes, then,' Haggard shouted.

'Don't let him,' said Florence suddenly. 'Stop him.'

He vented some of his anger on her, telling her to belt up and stay belted. She tried to pluck up courage to plead with him to take notice of her words, but failed. Her instinct told her that something terrible was about to happen to Haggard.

Haggard led the way into the bedroom. He pushed one of the doors of the built-in cupboard back along its guide rails with such force that it crashed against the end and rebounded.

Craig stared in silence at the clothes hanging in the cupboard.

'Well?' demanded Haggard.

Craig moved forward and examined the coats, sliding the hangers along the rail. He came to the Harris tweed sports jacket and held out one of the arms, the more closely to study the material.

Haggard reverted to elementary sarcasm once more. 'Specially made for me. Cost forty quid. Bit too rich for a split?'

'Yes, it is. It's a very distinctive coat.'

'That's nice of you to say that. Distinctive's a word I like. You know something, for a split you're almost educated. I'm beginning to like you.'

'I'm glad we're almost friends,' said Craig, as he unhooked the coat.

A kind of animal instinct, rather than Craig's actions, suddenly told Haggard that the time for amusing himself at the expense of the police was long since past. 'What are you doing?'

'Taking this coat away with us.'

'You ain't.'

'Don't panic. We'll give you a receipt for it.'

'You ain't taking that nowhere.'

'We'll have to. As far as I can judge, the material is exactly similar to the thread found on the door of the warehouse.'

'What warehouse?'

'The one where the job was done Saturday night.'

'There ain't no connection.'

Craig slid the coat off its hanger and folded it over his arms.

'You ain't taking that.'

'If you didn't do the job and so couldn't have been wearing this coat when you didn't do it, what are you panicking about?'

Haggard stared at Craig. Unaware of what he was doing, he reached up and touched the scar on his cheek. Craig hated his guts for what he'd done to that other split: yet Craig had meekly accepted all the insults that had been thrown at him. Looking back on the past quarter of an hour, Haggard suddenly recognised that there had been an air about Craig of . . . of expectant triumph. Triumph. Jesus! All the time he'd been jeering at this split, mocking him over Miller and family, the split had been working on him. 'You're trying to frame me,' he said, vicious anger flushing his face red.

'Frame you?' replied Craig, as if the word surprised him.

'You planted it.'

'Planted this coat here, in your bedroom? But you've only just told us how proud you are of it and how it cost so much more than any humble policeman could afford. D'you now want to deny it's yours?'

Haggard looked at the second detective. The man's expression was one of surprise, so clearly he didn't know what was going on. But Craig was smart. Far smarter than he looked. He hadn't come into this bedroom on his own, like Miller had. He'd come in with a witness so that in court he could sound as honest as George Washington. Of course the coat wasn't planted, but the thread in the warehouse had been. 'You were at the warehouse, weren't you?'

'Yes.'

'And I suppose you bleeding well found the thread?'

'No.'

Just for a second Haggard was baffled, but then the obvious

answer came to him. 'You planted the thread for someone else to find.'

'No.'

'I didn't do that job. I wouldn't touch it. You won't nail me, you bastard. I'll fix you. I'll fix you good and proper.'

'Like you fixed Miller?'

Haggard, using every ounce of self-control, tried to master his mercurial temper. Craig had planted the thread, which meant he had had to tear it off the coat first. So how'd he managed that? To his, Haggard's, knowledge, he'd never had the chance. Haggard swung round to speak to Florence. 'You've let him in?'

'No.'

Her denial infuriated him. 'You must have done, you stupid bitch.'

She flinched, as if she feared he was going to come across and strike her. 'I didn't.'

'I'll kill you,' he shouted wildly.

'I ain't never let him in. I swear it.'

Like some caged beast, Haggard swung back to face Craig. 'You bust in here when the place was empty and lifted the thread.'

Craig laughed.

Haggard jammed his right hand into his coat pocket. He longed, with a burning passion, for a cobbler's knife to stripe this split. He'd stripe him until his own mother would wonder what a bit of raw beef was doing on two legs. The Law wasn't going to get him for a job he hadn't done. He wouldn't have done that job, not if he was starving. A miserable thousand quid? They were trying to fix him. The bastards were trying to fix him. If only he'd had a knife. But maybe that's what they'd've liked. Maybe they'd been hoping he'd try to stripe one of them so as the two of 'em could jump him.

'D'you want to search the pockets before we give you a receipt for the coat?' asked Craig.

Haggard swore.

Craig emptied the pockets and put the contents on the bed. Nachton took a receipt form from the back of his notebook and filled it out. When he tried to hand it to Haggard, Haggard refused to take it so he dropped it on top of the things on the bed.

The detectives left.

Haggard swore with a wild panic. He crossed to where Florence stood. 'You let him in, didn't you? You were that stupid.'

She was terrified by his anger. 'I didn't.'

'You let him come in here and grab a thread from the coat?'

'I swear I didn't.'

He lit a cigarette. He was innocent. He was bloody innocent. He hadn't been within a thousand miles of the warehouse when it was done. They couldn't get him if he was innocent.

17

PERCY TRING, dressed in formal black coat and striped trousers, was shown into one of the prison interview-rooms in Frindhurst prison. The warder who had brought him there said that Haggard would be along almost immediately. Tring sat down at the bare wooden table and took the papers out of his brief-case. He held out his right hand, inspected his nails, and was annoyed to notice one of them was slightly dirty.

The door opened and Haggard and a warder came in. The warder said that when Tring was ready would he please ring the bell. The warder then left, shut the door, and locked it.

Haggard slammed his clenched fist down on the table. 'I didn't do that job. I'm innocent. D'you understand? I'm innocent.'

'All my clients are innocent.' Tring arranged the papers in front of himself.

'It couldn't have been me. I wouldn't do a twopenny-halfpenny job like this.'

'Whilst that may be very true, I fear it's not a line of defence we dare put before the jury, juries being notoriously narrow-minded.'

'I ain't hiring you to laugh at me.'

'You're not hiring me, you're instructing me, and I'm not laughing at you. Sit down.'

Haggard sat down.

'The police evidence that was given at the magistrates' court——' began Tring.

'They're framing me. I wasn't on that job. I was at home,

in bed. D'you think I'd waste my time on a kid's job? They're framing me. You've got to prove they're framing me.'

Tring pursed his lips. 'I have repeatedly told you that a defence along those lines can only be used once if it's to carry any weight.'

'But it's true.'

'I'm very sorry you're unable to understand.'

'I'm telling you I've been framed,' shouted Haggard wildly.

'No jury in this case will believe such a defence.'

'But it's bloody true.'

'So you have repeatedly said. Now, can we move on to discuss how we're going to present an effective plea in mitigation?'

Haggard's expression became one of horror. 'A plea—but that's for after a bloke's found guilty.'

'Quite so.'

'But I ain't going to be found guilty.'

'It might be better to treat the matter realistically.'

'I can't be found guilty. I didn't do it. You've got to prove I was framed.'

'Must I again tell you . . .'

Haggard told him where to put his advice.

Tring pursed his lips once more. He tapped his elegantly shaped fingers on the papers in front of himself. 'You really must try to control yourself.'

'Look, mate, if I go down, you'll go down with me. You control yourself on that one. I'll tell the Law just how things were fixed at my trial.'

'I don't know what you mean.'

'You know right enough.'

'Can you prove your wild assertions?'

'Not much I can't.'

'Are you quite certain?'

Haggard checked what he had been going to say and thought back to remember the manner in which the evidence at his trial had been faked. Tring had never done more than advise and had consistently refused to take an active part in what was going on. For the first time Haggard realised that there was absolutely no proof that Tring had played any part in the arrangements.

'Are you certain?' repeated Tring quietly.

'You dirty twister.'

'Self-preservation is one of the more active human attributes, as you will have learned at your last trial.'

Haggard clenched and unclenched his fists. 'But can't you bleeding well see?' he burst out. 'I didn't do that job. I can't be found guilty.'

'The one does not necessarily follow the other.'

'What's the law for if it ain't for getting the innocent off?'

'Why not ask Sergeant Miller?'

'To hell with Miller. It's me. I'm innocent.' Haggard fought for the one thing that remained constant. 'I've been framed. You've got to prove it.'

'I've warned you——'

'I said, you've got to prove it.'

'Very well.' Tring pursed his lips. 'I cannot force you to accept my considered advice.'

·   ·   ·   ·   ·

Florence visited Haggard that afternoon. She was taken to the Visiting Room, a long rectangular room, completely institutional, with a table right down its centre. A glass partition, four feet high, stood on the table and below was a solid partition from table to floor. In the glass partition, opposite the chairs, were speaking places of the design found at railway stations.

Haggard was escorted into the room. When he saw Florence he began to walk with a swagger. He sat down in the chair opposite hers, took a packet of cigarettes from his pocket, and lit one.

The warder leaned against the door and stared with lascivious appreciation at Florence.

'How are things?' asked Florence, in little more than a whisper.

He studied her. Her eyes were red and puffy, meaning she'd

been crying recently. It made him feel good to know a brass had been crying for him. 'I'll live,' he said.

'What . . . what did the mouthpiece say?'

'That stupid bastard.'

'He will get you off, won't he?'

'Lawyers make me puke.'

'Does he believe you?'

'What's it matter?'

'But you've got to tell me, does he believe you?'

He wondered what in the hell was biting her? What had she got to get excited about? She was all right: she was outside. She could go into the streets and walk along them, look up and see the sky.

'Please, Tom, does he believe you?'

'Him? He wouldn't believe himself.'

'He's got to be made to believe you.'

She was being bright, she was! The mouthpiece had to believe him, she said. What the mouthpiece believed was of as much importance as a duke's spit: it was the jury he had to get excited about. They must believe him. Everyone knew that juries were there to believe the truth. He was innocent. They couldn't put him inside on P.D. for a job he hadn't done. It could be ten years. That was what was staring him in the face. Ten years locked away so that the world outside became so dim it ceased to exist in reality. After ten years a man wasn't with it: he wasn't with anything. They couldn't do that to him, for a job he hadn't done.

'Tom, I . . . You . . . I've got to tell you.'

Got to tell him? That the moon was round, lawyers were crooked, and stockbrokers were kinky?

'He did take it, Tom.'

He stared at her. She was all excited and she didn't make sense. She used to get excited in bed: by God, she did. As he remembered what they'd done together when he'd been outside, bitterness and anger seemed like icy fingers pressing into his throat.

'The split took it then,' she said.

'Took what?'

165

'The bit from your coat.'

His voice became rough. 'You said he wasn't never in the flat.'

'I didn't dare say. He . . . he said you was out with a spade. He said you met her just outside the flat. I couldn't bear to think of it. It made me feel sick. When he said you met her just outside, I had to do something to hurt you.'

His brain seemed to have been slowed down already by his stay in custody. He heard the words, but it took time for them to arrange themselves into a meaning.

'I was too scared to tell you, Tom. I knew it'd make you hate me and I couldn't have you hating me. I made him wear the coat so as to . . . And that's when he must have taken the thread. I had to do it because he said you was out with a spade.'

Waves of anger washed through his mind. She'd landed him in this stinking mess. She'd taken a split into their bed. That was the way she'd repaid all the kindness he'd shown her. She'd let the split use his bed. She'd given the split every chance in the world to make the frame. Haggard clenched his fists.

He stood up, kicked the chair backwards, and vaulted up on to the table. The warder shouted and began to blow his whistle. Haggard scrambled over the glass barrier and jumped down on to the floor. She sat quite still in the chair.

He tried to throttle her, but the warder prevented him. A second warder ran into the room and they managed to drag him away from her. He struggled so wildly that just for a moment it seemed he'd break free and so be able to smash this brass who'd betrayed him, but a third warder arrived and between them they finally overpowered him.

Tears spilled down her cheeks. 'I only did it because I loved you and he said you was out with a spade,' she whispered.

.   .   .   .   .

Haggard's trial opened on the morning of 17th October. Craig went into the witness-box immediately after lunch. His examination-in-chief lasted just over half an hour.

Defence counsel prepared to cross-examine. He lifted his wig, scratched his bald head, dropped the wig back into place and flicked the tails clear of his neck. He was one of the ugliest men at the Bar, yet his personality was such that listeners were almost unaware of his ugliness. 'Constable, you categorically deny you visited the accused's flat between the dates in question?'

'Yes, sir.'

'You do realise the importance of your answer?'

'Yes, sir.'

'You don't wish to add or subtract anything to what you've said?'

'No, sir.'

'It is only fair at this point to tell you that I shall be calling a witness who will testify that you are lying.'

Craig made no answer.

'Have you nothing to say to that?'

'I am not lying, sir.'

'You deny it. Very well. Tell me, do you consider that a policeman's duty is to bring a guilty man to trial?'

'I believe a policeman's duty is thoroughly to investigate the evidence, sir, whether the evidence is for or against the person concerned.'

'A pious observation.'

'And a very correct one,' said the judge.

Counsel bowed, ironically, at the Bench. He turned back. 'Constable, I am going to call a witness, Miss Florence Jones, who will say that in Haggard's flat you falsely told her Haggard was out with a coloured woman. She will go on to say that because of this jealousy she invited you into the bedroom that she and the accused man, Haggard, occupied. There she persuaded you to wear one of Haggard's coats for a while and the one you chose was a Harris tweed sports coat, brown with yellow speckles, the coat that is exhibit number seven in court today. Is all that true?'

'No, sir.'

'Let us take it seriatim. Did you tell Miss Florence Jones that Haggard was out with a coloured woman?'

'No, sir.'
'Did you go to the bedroom with her?'
'No, sir.'
'Did you wear the coat, exhibit number seven?'
'No, sir.'
'Did you have sexual intercourse with her?'
'No, sir.'
'Constable, do you really expect the court to believe that the young lady I shall be calling would have made up a story of this character?'
'She obviously did, sir.'
'Not obviously, not if you're lying from beginning to end.'
'I'm telling the truth.'
'If her story is correct, we have a very clear picture of how you obtained the thread from the coat, don't we?'
'I wouldn't know, sir.'
'Why not?'
'I wouldn't know how you can manage to get any kind of a picture, sir.'
'Don't be impertinent.'
The judge intervened. 'I fail to see any degree of impertinence in this witness's reply.'
'My Lord, I'm tempted to misquote and say that impertinence lies in the ears of the listener.'
'And any listener can be just as wrongly biased as any beholder who sees beauty where it does not exist.'
Counsel addressed Craig again. 'Have you ever worked with a fellow detective who has been found guilty of perjury?'
'I have.'
'What was that detective's name?'
'Sergeant Miller.'
'Was he found guilty of planting faked evidence on someone?'
'Yes, sir.'
'On whom?'
'Haggard.'
'The accused in the present case?'
'Yes, sir.'

'Was Miller a friend of yours as well as a colleague?'
'Yes.'
'Then it must have upset you when he was tried and found guilty?'
'It did.'
'Do you believe Sergeant Miller was innocent of what he was accused of?'
'I do.'
'Whom do you believe was lying at that trial? Haggard?'
'Haggard was lying.'
'You must have hated him, then?'
'In a way.'
'In every way, I suggest. If you had wanted to gain revenge on Haggard, how would you have gone about it?'
'I've no idea.'
'Wouldn't you have decided that by far the best way would be to incriminate him by planting false evidence, just as Sergeant Miller had done?'
'How do I know what I'd have decided as I didn't decide anything?'
'But I say you did, Constable. I say you decided falsely to incriminate Haggard in this warehouse robbery.'

The judge intervened once more. 'I think you have sufficiently made your point.'

'My Lord, what I am attempting to do . . .'

'I am certain we are all well aware of what you are attempting to do, even if some of us are uncertain as to the advisability of it.'

Craig looked at the dock. Haggard stared back at him, his face contorted by an expression of hatred.

. . . . .

Florence, when she gave her evidence-in-chief, looked so defenceless and so easily hurt that more than one person felt possessively sorry for her. Prosecuting counsel, by his cross-examination, made it quite clear that he was not one of these.

'Let us examine your evidence a little more closely, Miss Jones.'

He was a bean-pole of a man who looked as if he needed a succession of square meals. 'You claim that the accused left the flat on the morning in question about ten minutes before Detective Constable Craig arrived?'

'Yes,' she said, in a low voice.

'Did you like Constable Craig?'

She went to speak, realised that to answer either yes or no was to entrap herself, and said nothing.

'Miss Jones, isn't the truth that you hated him?'

'Not hated.'

'But you testified to my learned friend only a short while ago that you believed he was falsely trying to incriminate the accused, Haggard?'

She recognised that it was absurd to try to deny her true feelings. 'All right. I hated him.'

'Then why let him into the flat?'

'Why?'

'That is the question.'

'He forced his way in.'

'Are you now trying to claim that he used physical force?'

'No.'

'Then what are you trying to say?'

'It was the way he spoke. I'd never have let him in if he hadn't talked about Tom.'

'What did he say?'

'He told me Tom was out with a woman.'

'But just now you claimed it was only after he was in the hall of the flat that he spoke about this woman.'

'I'm . . . I'm telling the truth.'

'Which version is the truth, Miss Jones?'

'Please, please, it's the truth. You've got to believe me.'

'It is the jury whom you must try to convince, not me.' Counsel waited, but when she said nothing more he continued. 'You have testified that you gave Constable Craig a drink—even though you hated him—and that he then told you all about this coloured woman the accused was supposed to be out with. You became so jealous you called the constable into the bedroom, made him wear the accused's coat, and called the constable to bed with you. Are you still claiming this is the truth?'

'But it is the truth.'

'I wonder if you can explain to the jury why you offered such —intimate—hospitality to a man whom you hated so much?'

'Why can't you understand? He lied to me about the woman. He made me think Tom was with a spade from the same town. I knew he had women in London, but that wasn't the same. It didn't matter what he did in London, but in Telton it was like . . . like using our bed. It made me mad with jealousy. I love Tom. When I thought he was out with a coloured in the same town, I had to hurt him. That's why I made the detective dress in his coat and then . . . then . . .'

'Indulge in sexual intercourse?'

'Yes.'

'Your story, Miss Jones, is an extraordinary one, but I don't suppose many people will disagree with me when I confess that I find by far the most extraordinary thing about it is the way you would have us believe you so casually seduced Constable Craig, as if this act were of no physical account.'

'But it wasn't.'

'Not? Do you really ask the jury to believe that?' asked counsel, with bland amazement.

'It didn't mean nothing because . . .' She stopped.

'Because?'

She knew that the admission must damage her standing as a witness, but not to make it now that she had been tricked into the position in which she found herself would be even more damaging. 'I'm . . . I'm on the streets.'

'What precisely do you mean by that?'

'I'm a prostitute. But not when I'm with him,' she said desperately.

'Not what?'

'I'm not on the streets.'

'I'm sure the accused appreciates your consideration.'

'But you won't understand. I love him.'

'Is that why you stop plying your trade when you and he are living together?'

'Yes.'

'But don't you say that, while still living with the accused, you plied it with Constable Craig?'

'That's not true.'

'Miss Jones, it is you who claim to have had sexual intercourse with Constable Craig.'

'But I wasn't plying my trade. I didn't do it for money.'

'I'm sorry. I'm not really conversant with the niceties of the situation.'

'Please . . . please, I love him.'

'So you have said several times.'

Desperately she fought to make them understand that a woman like her could love. 'I've always loved him. I'd do anything for him, anything. I wouldn't care what it was. That's how much I love him. He could kick me to death and I'd still love him. If he told me to do anything at all, I'd do it.'

'Such as coming to this court and lying?'

She stared aghast at counsel. She had exposed her soul in the desperate struggle to convince them of the truth and the only result was to increase their scorn. Tears gathered in her eyes.

Prosecuting counsel studied the jury. The men were looking at the witness with varying degrees of lascivious interest and the two middle-aged women were tight-lipped. There was no need to pursue any of the points raised. He picked up his notebook and read through some of his notes. He put the notebook down. 'I am sure we will all try not to be prejudiced by what you have said.' He allowed a long pause for the forces of prejudice to increase. 'Miss Jones, you have not answered one very important question. Why should Constable Craig have tried to frame the accused?'

'In revenge.'

'In revenge for what?'

She was so desperate that she could think only of the need to convince them of the truth. She spoke wildly. 'In revenge for Tom fixing the case, that's what.'

Haggard began to curse her, shouting wildly.

. . . . .

The judge, in his summing-up, repeatedly made it clear what he thought the verdict should be.

'Members of the jury, you have all heard the evidence of Miss Jones who, in the witness-box, admitted to being a prostitute who was living with the accused. As men and women of the world, you will not allow your repugnance for such a situation to colour the manner in which you receive her evidence. A woman of no morals is capable of telling the truth. However, it is only fair to direct you that when two persons give contradictory evidence and you have to decide which one to believe, you are entitled to take account of the character of these two witnesses. In this respect, you must decide what weight you will give to the evidence of a woman who claims that while living with one man she went out of her way to have sexual intercourse with another man. You heard Miss Jones frequently protest her love for the accused. You may well wonder what she means by the word "love" . . .'

. . . . .

'Guilty,' said the foreman of the jury.

There was a general shuffling of feet and clearing of throats.

Haggard's list of previous convictions was read out and he was asked if he had anything to say before sentence was delivered.

'I'm innocent,' he shouted wildly. 'I'm innocent. He framed me.'

'You do yourself no good by these wild outbursts,' said the judge. 'Thomas Haggard, you have rightly been found guilty of a despicable and brutal crime. You, and two others as yet unknown, carried out a robbery in the course of which you severely injured an elderly man through the casual use of violence. I intend to make it quite clear that these courts have no intention of allowing the wave of violence to go unchecked. I sentence you to twelve years 'preventive detention.'

Haggard began to shout, but the two warders managed to quieten him.

'During the course of this trial,' continued the judge, 'a deliberate and wicked attack was made on the character of Detective Constable Craig. I wish to make it quite clear that this court finds such attack totally unfounded. Detective Constable Craig did not visit the flat as has been alleged, nor did he falsify any of the evidence. His character remains completely unsullied.

'A witness, Miss Jones, admitted on oath that evidence previously given in a court of law was false. I direct that this statement be brought to the attention of the proper authorities for immediate investigation.'

18

THE highly polished Austin Westminster came to a halt in front of Breen's house and Radamski climbed out. He thanked the constable who was driving, gave the time he wanted to be picked up, and turned and went across to the front door. He rang the bell. As he waited, he stared at the new Rolls-Royce, parked on the far side of the drive. Breen had the money to live luxuriously and did so. Radamski agreed with that—he had nothing but contempt for the wealthy man who chose to lead a frugal life.

The German girl opened the door and smilingly wished him a good morning. She showed him into the sitting-room where Breen and his wife were waiting.

'What will you drink, Charles?' asked Breen. 'Would you care to risk a Polaris, which is Campari, Vermouth, a touch of brandy, and soda?'

'I'd like to try it if I may.' He smiled. 'My life insurance is in good order.'

While her husband mixed the drinks, Vera Breen and Radamski discussed the new flower bed she was proposing to have made.

Breen handed the glasses round. The two men smoked. After some five minutes, Vera Breen stood up and said she must go and check that all was well with the meal. 'We've escallop of veal, Charles. I do hope you like it?'

'It's almost my favourite dish.'

She smiled, a trifle shyly. 'I'm so glad. You're very rewarding to give a meal to and not at all like Reggie. If I gave him sausages and mash every day of the week, he wouldn't notice.'

175

'That's malicious nonsense,' said Breen lightly. 'This, Charles, you must understand is my punishment for daring to criticise something we had last week which was a trifle burnt.'

'It was not in the least burnt,' she denied. 'One of these days I'll really burn something so that you can know what it's like.' She left the room and carefully closed the door behind her.

Breen settled back in the arm-chair. 'How are things, Charles?'

'I've had a letter from the Home Secretary's office.'

'About the trial?'

'Yes. More accurately, about all three trials.'

'Well, we rather expected something, didn't we?'

'Not exactly in these tones, though.' Radamski took a letter from his inside breast pocket and passed it across.

Breen read the letter. He looked up. 'It is rather sharp.' He finished his drink.

'We did our best.'

'Your force always does do its best, Charles, and I don't mind telling you that the whole of the Watch Committee recognises the fact. It wouldn't do any harm for the committee to write to the Home Secretary and tell him just that, would it?'

'It would certainly be a great help.'

'I think we'll take the opportunity at the same time to point out just how extensive your enquiries were. We're not going to give the Home Secretary a chance to run down the efficiency of the Frindhurst police.' Breen stood up. 'Let me give you a refill?'

'Thanks very much. It's rather a good drink.' Radamski passed over his glass.

Breen did not speak again until he had returned to his chair. 'I think we ought to have a quick word about the future, Charles. You'll naturally be making the most extensive enquiries into the possibility of Haggard's having faked the evidence against Sergeant Miller?'

'Yes, of course.'

'The statement of that woman Jones at Haggard's last trial must show what probably happened. In the circumstances, it's obviously up to the Frindhurst police to move heaven and earth to uncover the evidence of Sergeant Miller's innocence.'

'I couldn't agree more.'

'I knew that's how you'd feel. I don't want to sound melodramatic, but I think it's right to say that our police force is in many ways itself on trial. If it finds the proof of Miller's innocence, then it will have passed the trial with flying colours. Once we have shown how efficient we are, we need not fear any order for amalgamation with the county police force, under the 'sixty-four Act, nor need we fear the influence of R.C.S.'

'If it's humanly possible, we'll uncover the evidence.'

'You know, Charles, I really do wish that all those who shout so loudly for a national police force could see our city in action and be made to realise what priceless thing would be lost if the local liaison, born of local pride, no longer existed.' Breen raised his glass. 'Let's drink to success, Charles, success that will prove the worth of all we fight for.'

. . . . . .

Detective Inspector Everam was an intelligent, ambitious man who knew how far he could afford to push his luck and when it would pay him to go right up to that limit. He and his detective sergeant went to Carpenter's house one evening. Carpenter showed them into the sitting-room.

Carpenter's beady eyes looked from one detective to another. He could not conceal his nervousness. 'Please sit down, gentlemen. Can I offer you a beer? It's a very warm night.'

The D.I. made no move towards the chairs. 'Nothing,' he replied.

'And the other——'

'I said, nothing.'

'Then . . . D'you mind, like, if I have one?'

'I can't stop you.'

Carpenter hurried out of the room and returned in less than

half a minute with a glass tumbler full of beer. The tumbler shook.

'You'd better sit down,' said the D.I.

'Yes, of course. Just wanted to see you'd got everything you needed.'

'Sit down.'

Carpenter sat down on a pouf.

There was a silence. Carpenter drank quickly and beer trickled down the sides of his mouth. He began to fidget, nervously tapping his knees with the fingers of his right hand. Finally, he had to speak. 'What's up, then?'

'What's up?' The D.I. repeated the question with contemptuous surprise.

'Well, I don't know, do I?'

The detective sergeant spoke in a mild and friendly voice. 'You must do.' His manner was in very marked contrast to his superior's.

'Why must I?'

'You read the papers, chum.'

'No . . . I mean, I read 'em, but there's been nothing to concern me.'

'Have you seen the report on the trial of Haggard?' snapped the D.I.

'I . . . That is . . . Yes.'

'The woman swears the evidence in the first trial was faked.'

'That's a lie,' said Carpenter hoarsely. 'I told the truth. I recognised the glove. I sold it . . .'

'Do you know the penalties for perjury?'

'They don't concern me none.'

'They concern you intimately. The glove was not bought in your shop and nor did you ever see Miller in it.'

'But I swear I did.'

The D.I. ignored the answer. There was another silence. Carpenter finished his beer with noisy gulps.

The detective sergeant took up the questioning, in a friendly, fellow-to-fellow, manner. 'We're here to help you.'

'I don't need no help.'

'But that's just what you do need. You see, you can do one

of two things now the truth's come out in open court. You can decide either to hurry up and tell the truth yourself and leave us to do our best for you in the way of a recommendation for mercy, or you can go on lying all the way to court when you'll go down on a very nasty perjury and conspiracy charge.'

'I didn't . . .'

'You're new to a racket like this one, aren't you? You've no idea how a real villain like Haggard works. When he gets in trouble he does anything he can to get out of it and that includes singing as hard as any canary. He chucks everyone else overboard just in the hope that leaves him with his feet high and dry. You don't really believe that Haggard hasn't already talked, do you?'

'He . . . he hasn't anything to talk about that could worry me.'

The D.I. laughed sarcastically.

'We're only trying to help you,' said the detective sergeant reproachfully.

'It don't concern me. I swear it don't.'

The D.I. walked across to the door. 'We're wasting our time.' He opened the door.

The detective sergeant spoke in a low voice to Carpenter. 'Haggard's solicitor has made a full confession, chum, and put your neck right in the noose. Haggard's talked and put everything on your shoulders.'

The D.I. went out of the room.

The detective sergeant jerked his thumb at the half-closed door. 'He came here to help you, but now you've turned him down he'll get real mean. He can be the meanest bastard I know.'

Carpenter was so scared he found difficulty in swallowing.

The D.I. called out from the hall. 'Leave him to it. If he's asking to do ten years, leave him to it.'

'Ten . . . ten years?' mumbled Carpenter.

'This case is a big one.'

'But ten years . . .'

'Life gets rough when you play it rough. You were given

just one chance and look what you've done with it. Turned it down flat. Still, it's your funeral, not mine.'

The D.I. shouted from outside again. 'Come on, man.'

'But I can't say anything now,' muttered Carpenter wildly, 'not after what I said in court.'

'But look what that Jones woman said. Where d'you think that puts you?' The detective sergeant continued to speak to Carpenter in a sympathetic manner. Soon, the D.I. would return to the room and he'd swear, shout, and threaten Carpenter with everything in the book. Between them, using the age-old strategem of one pleasant and one unpleasant interrogator, mixing threats with promises, they'd go on working on Carpenter. It looked as if they would sooner or later break him and gain the confession they so desperately needed.

. . . . . .

For twenty-four hours after he was released from prison, Albert Miller treated life as a miracle. He stared up at the blue sky in wonderment, viewed his wife as a possible mirage, and kept reminding himself that at any moment he would wake up in the cell and see the other two men who hated his guts because he was a busted split. But he was too matter-of-fact in his make-up for this sense of bewilderment and heightened perception to last. After the twenty-four hours were over, the world outside had become the real and ordinary one and the world inside the prison became the bad dream.

Violet Miller waited until the second day to give him the special victory meal. She bought the kind of food and drink that they had on very special occasions, such as wedding anniversaries. Potted shrimps, large fillet steaks from the best butcher in Frindhurst, as many chips as Albert could eat and to the devil with a bulging waistline, and real sherry trifle smothered under whipped cream. There were bottles of sherry, whisky, red wine, and port. If Albert got so tight he couldn't remember his own name, so what? If a wife couldn't let a man get tight at such a moment, she wasn't much of a wife.

Craig was asked to their victory meal. He refused the

invitation until he realised how deeply Violet was hurt by his refusal and then he accepted, making some excuse that until then he had thought they would want to be on their own.

He left his digs at six-thirty in the evening. The landlady appeared as he opened the front door and aggressively demanded to know whether he would be late. He said he was going out to raid a brothel and therefore didn't know how long he'd be. For once, he was allowed the last word.

He walked slowly along the pavement. He passed a woman pushing a pram and she looked vaguely like Daphne. An express letter from Daphne had come that morning and it was in his breast pocket. Why hadn't he written to her? Surely, he didn't think for one second she believed a single word that that horrible tart had said in court? She was in love with him, which meant that she knew—underlined three times—he could never have done such a thing as sleep with so common a slut. He had written an answer half an hour ago. He had gone into the flat, he had undressed the woman, he had had her on the bed. Florence might be a tart, but she wasn't a slut. No one who could love as she loved could be a slut. He'd torn up the letter. Why had he tried to confess? A confession like that one would never do anything but harm. Was he seeking the solace of confessional degradation? Confessions were for the women's magazines in which there were not allowed to be any bitter aftermaths when memory returned again and again.

If he were put in the same position again, what would he do? Would he follow Florence into the bedroom? If he hadn't followed her, Dusty wouldn't be free: if he hadn't followed her, he would have retained his own integrity. The guilty man had now been punished and the innocent man set free, but had justice been done? What means were lawful to free a man unlawfully imprisoned: what means were lawful to imprison a man unlawfully free?

He reached the end of the street and had to wait for the traffic to ease before he could cross the road. A vintage Bentley went past, huge exhaust booming, the driver complete with R.A.F. moustache and a beautiful woman in the passenger seat. Money, he thought, was the really important thing in life. One didn't need integrity if one was a millionaire.

He came within sight of Miller's house and slowed his already slow rate of walking. There was a second confession he wanted to make. 'Dusty, I lied, cheated, perverted the course of the law if not of justice, denied the trust placed in me as a policeman, dishonoured my oath of loyalty, all to free you. Was I right? Is human injustice the greatest sin on earth?' But he would say nothing because Dusty would understand nothing.

He came to the house and knocked on the front door. Violet Miller opened it. 'I knew it would be you so I told Mrs. Hubble not to worry.' Her voice was loud and quick and because she held a glass in her hand he at first thought she was already tiddly, but he corrected himself immediately. She was only drunk on happiness.

They went through to the small sitting-room. The children excitedly greeted him and Dusty offered him anything he wanted in the way of a drink, provided it was whisky or sherry. He chose whisky.

When they each had a glass, Miller raised his. 'To my lucky stars,' he said.

'They weren't all that lucky for a long time,' said Violet, almost with annoyance.

He drank before he answered. 'Suppose Haggard hadn't done another job—where should I be now? Still in cell B sixty-one.' He turned. 'And you, John, you had your lucky stars, too, didn't you?'

'Did I?' answered Craig.

'I'll say you did. That charge of fixing the evidence never began to stick on you.'

'I suppose it didn't.'

'What in the hell made Haggard try a second time?'

'He thought he was on to a good thing.'

Miller spoke boisterously. 'Why so glum, chum? Sorry I'm coming back to the office to boss you around?' He laughed loudly. 'I suppose you didn't fix the evidence? Eh?'

'No,' said Craig.

'Then drink up and start looking cheerful. The bottom of the glass is all I intend to study this evening.' He winked. 'After we've got rid of the kids, we'll see just how quickly we can make all these bottles look sick. So here's damnation to villains.'

They drank.

If you have enjoyed this book, you might wish to join the Walker British Mystery Society.

For information, please send a postcard or letter to:

Paperback Mystery Editor

**Walker & Company
720 Fifth Avenue
New York, NY 10019**